Rathe stood, un[...] **the chair as though afraid she might bolt.**

But bolting was the last thing on her mind as she identified the heady, racing sensation that had pounded through her during the fight. Excitement. This was the adventure she craved, the thrill she'd been seeking.

The adrenaline poured through her body. She wanted to run. She wanted to dance, to sing, to tip her head back and scream.

She grinned at Rathe.

His eyes narrowing, he advanced on her and leaned down so they were face-to-face. "This is not a joke, Nia. Don't you get it? You could've been killed," he said, then placed a palm flat against the door, effectively trapping her.

"Well, I wasn't, thanks to you. That's why the doctors here work in teams, remember? So we can watch each other's backs." She shoved at his chest with both hands, but he was immovable. "Damn it, let me go!"

She saw the change in his eyes. Her body answered the call and he bent close and whispered, "I can't."

Then he kissed her, and all that restless energy redirected itself to the places where their bodies merged.

Dear Harlequin Intrigue Reader,

Spring is in the air and we have a month of fabulous books for you to curl up with as the March winds howl outside:

- Familiar is back on the prowl, in Caroline Burnes's *Familiar Texas*. And *Rocky Mountain Maneuvers* marks the conclusion of Cassie Miles's COLORADO CRIME CONSULTANTS trilogy.

- Jessica Andersen brings us an exciting medical thriller, *Covert M.D.*

- Don't miss the next ECLIPSE title, Lisa Childs's *The Substitute Sister*.

- Definitely check out our April lineup. Debra Webb is starting THE ENFORCERS, an exciting new miniseries you won't want to miss. Also look for a special 3-in-1 story from Rebecca York, Ann Voss Peterson and Patricia Rosemoor called *Desert Sons*.

Each month, Harlequin Intrigue brings you a variety of heart-stopping romantic suspense and chilling mystery. Don't miss a single book!

Sincerely,

Denise O'Sullivan
Senior Editor
Harlequin Intrigue

COVERT M.D.
JESSICA ANDERSEN

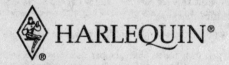

HARLEQUIN®

TORONTO • NEW YORK • LONDON
AMSTERDAM • PARIS • SYDNEY • HAMBURG
STOCKHOLM • ATHENS • TOKYO • MILAN • MADRID
PRAGUE • WARSAW • BUDAPEST • AUCKLAND

To my friends in the New England Chapter
of Romance Writers of America.

ISBN 0-373-22833-3

COVERT M.D.

www.eHarlequin.com

Printed in U.S.A.

ABOUT THE AUTHOR

Though she's tried out professions ranging from cleaning sea lion cages to cloning glaucoma genes, from patent law to training horses—Jessica is happiest when she's combining all these interests with her first love: writing romances. These days she's delighted to be writing full-time on a farm in rural Connecticut that she shares with a small menagerie and a hero named Brian. She hopes you'll visit her at www.JessicaAndersen.com for info on upcoming books, contests and to say "hi"!

Books by Jessica Andersen

Don't miss any of our special offers. Write to us at the following address for information on our newest releases.

Harlequin Reader Service
U.S.: 3010 Walden Ave., P.O. Box 1325, Buffalo, NY 14269
Canadian: P.O. Box 609, Fort Erie, Ont. L2A 5X3

CAST OF CHARACTERS

Dr. Nia French—Nia and her first lover are partnered in a deadly hospital investigation of failed transplants. Will she learn to forgive him before it's too late?

Dr. Rathe McKay—The guarded doctor-adventurer has two equally difficult tasks: to protect Nia from a vicious killer and to avoid the chemistry between them.

Cadaver Man—The tall, gray man sees through Nia and Rathe's covers quickly. Too quickly.

Tony French—Nia's father drove Rathe off years ago. After his death, will Tony's memory separate the onetime lovers or bring them closer together as danger escalates?

Dr. Logan Hart—The young transplant specialist wants to assist in the investigation of unexpected patient deaths. Or so he says.

Marissa Doyle—The nurse has overseen many of the dead patients and has hidden secrets.

Dr. Michael Talbot—The head of the transplant department, Talbot is a giant within the field. So why is a killer stalking his patients?

Short Whiny Guy—Cadaver Man's partner has seen too much.

Chapter One

The damp subbasement of Boston General Hospital smelled faintly of death and fabric softener. Corridors folded back on each other without apparent reason, which was both a blessing and a curse for Nia French.

A blessing because she was able to stay out of sight. A curse because she had to follow close or risk losing Cadaver Man, Short Whiny Guy and the rattling laundry cart.

"You got the keys?"

Nia froze. The voice was near. Too near.

Heart pounding, she breathed through her mouth and eased closer to the off-green cinder block wall, wishing for some cover. Wishing the fluorescent lights weren't so relentlessly bright.

Wishing she knew for sure she'd followed the right guys.

"Yeah, I got the keys. Why, you think I lost them already?" The second speaker was Short Whiny Guy, who had complained incessantly during the trip down from the sixth floor. There was a metallic jingle, and the sound of a door being unlocked.

"Just shut up and let's get this thing loaded," Cadaver Man ordered. She called him that because of the grayish skin and shadowed eyes she'd glimpsed when the elevators had shut on the men, leaving her wondering why they were changing the linens at two in the morning.

And why none of the beds in the Transplant Department were stripped.

Nia had followed them because this was her first assignment in HFH's Investigations Division, and she was determined to prove herself.

Her previous assignments for Hospitals for Humanity had sent her to outbreaks and disaster areas worldwide, where her medical degree made her useful and her guts were taken for granted. It was good work, but it wasn't where her heart lay. More than anything, she wanted to be an investigator—and now, finally, she'd been given the opportunity to work a case.

Hearing a metal door slide open and the men's voices move away, Nia crouched down and eased around the corner, forcing her hands not to tremble from a mixture of nerves and excitement.

In contrast to the rest of the hospital, the loading bay was dark. The smell here was stronger, both of decay and of fabric softener, though the wide garage door let in a thin breath of Chinatown funk.

The men were gone. The big laundry hamper they had wheeled down from the sixth floor sat on the loading dock.

"Transplants failing for no good reason," the dossier on this assignment read. "Supplies and pharmaceuticals disappearing from the Transplant Unit."

Though the assignment didn't officially begin until the next day, when she'd meet her new partner and they would be briefed on the full scope of the problem, Nia had sneaked into the hospital at midnight. She'd been hoping to discover something useful. Hoping to get a head start on impressing the senior investigator HFH had assigned to train her.

And here was her chance.

Stepping quietly on her soft-soled sneakers, she eased around the corner and crept toward the hamper. She had no concrete reason to suspect there was anything inside but laundry. But her left eyelid had twitched a warning, and the shift schedule indicated the linens in the Transplant Department were changed at seven in the morning, not two. Holding her breath, she stood on her tiptoes and peered inside the tall hamper.

It was full of laundry.

"Damn it," she muttered under her breath, "why can't they make these things shorter?" Twenty-eight-year-old Nia had topped out at five-two. Usually she could mask her short stature with determination, but the hamper didn't care how tough she was, it still came up past her breasts. She had two choices—dive in and hope for the best or hang back and wait.

The sound of an engine and the rhythmic beep of a truck backing into the loading dock told her that "wait" was the better option. Darting behind a half-open door, she pressed her eye to the crack by the hinge and congratulated herself on a fine hiding spot.

She'd be a good investigator. No matter what *certain people* thought, she was going to make it. It had been her dream for nearly ten years now, ever since she'd first heard the stories about a swashbuckling HFH doctor saving the world.

"Come on, let's get it loaded and get out of here. This stuff gives me the creeps." Short Whiny Guy's voice preceded him onto the loading dock. Cadaver Man, looking grayer in the half-light, unlatched the back of the laundry truck and ran up the door. Nia froze.

That was no laundry truck.

An empty gurney was secured to one side. Equipment sprouted from every flat surface and dangled from the ceiling. A faint white mist wafted out, as though the air-conditioning had been turned from "chill" to "preserve."

"Ay-uh. We wouldn't want to keep him waiting for his things, would we?" Cadaver Man, who hadn't spoken up to this point, gave a ghastly grin that was at odds with his down-home Maine accent.

Nia's pulse raced. Her first night on the job and she already had a huge break. If she got on that van and figured out where it was headed, what it was doing, then she could solve the case in a single night.

Score one for Nia French.

Short Whiny Guy pushed the laundry hamper across a narrow ramp and into the cleared center of the cargo area. The cart's dirty canvas and worn wheels looked incongruous amidst so much stainless-steel and high-tech equipment.

"Come on, guys, give me a break here," Nia whispered, her burst of optimism draining when Short Whiny Guy climbed into the back with the laundry hamper, as though it was his job to watch over the dirty linens. Cadaver Man shut the door and latched it securely.

Damn. Now what was she going to do? Her car was parked in the main garage on the other side of the hospital, so there was no way she could follow the men. Unless…

Her eyes narrowed on the back bumper of the van, which was fitted with a hydraulic cargo lift. The lift was wide and flat, with plenty of hand holds. She could jump right on.

She touched her back pocket and was reassured by the shape of her miniature tool kit. Given the chance, she might even be able to get the van open.

Cadaver Man reached up and pulled the loading dock's garage door down, but the vehicle was still visible through a smaller opening nearby.

Nia's heart pounded as the van's engine started up. She rubbed her sweaty palms against her dark jeans and slipped out from the hiding spot.

"I can do this," she said, reaching for the latch of the outer door as Cadaver Man ground the gears, searching for first. "I can do this. I can—"

"Oh, no you don't!" Rough hands grabbed Nia, spun her and shoved her up against the wall, into the deep shadows. She panicked and screeched in terror.

Her assailant was taller than she, though only by seven

or eight inches, and his rangy body jostled against hers as they struggled. She shoved against him. "Let me go!"

Oh, God, had she missed a third man? Panic spurted through her veins, and she shot an elbow at her attacker's chin in a one-two move that her self-defense instructor had assured her should be followed by a knee to the groin.

Her captor blocked the elbow, but his grip slackened. "Nadia?"

She knew his voice instantly, but it was too late to stop the "two" of her one-two attack. She kneed him right where it hurt. Hard.

Rathe McKay, the most famous of HFH's investigators—and Nia's first lover—went pale, sank to the floor and wheezed.

Outside, the van revved and pulled away, its occupants unaware of the scuffle behind them on the loading dock.

Nia stood, stunned, as emotions battled within her. Guilt that she'd hurt him. Confusion as to why he'd sneaked up on her and why he was even in the hospital. And above all else, excitement at seeing him again after all this time.

Although his desertion had nearly destroyed her before, he still had the ability to leave her breathless. Because, damn it, even curled up on the floor, swearing, Rathe McKay looked good to her. Real good.

His close-cropped hair was lighter than she remembered, prematurely silver, though he was only thirty-eight. The seven years since she'd last seen him had added new lines to his angular face, making him look older than his calendar age even as they added to his appeal. His wide shoulders and chest spoke of coiled energy, and his arms and legs still boasted the leashed power she remembered, the grace that could carry him soundlessly through rainforests or dance him elegantly through the classiest ballroom.

And his eyes, when he opened them, still stared through her as though he could see into her soul.

"Rathe, I'm so sorry—" Horrified guilt swamped the shock. She offered a hand, but paused when a terrible possibility occurred. She withdrew her hand. "What are you doing here?"

He scowled, though something else moved in his eyes. Surprise, maybe, or wariness. Then those abstract emotions were gone, blanked out by the familiar stoniness. "I should've known something was wrong when Wainwright wouldn't tell me who I'd be training."

Rathe was her mentor? No. Impossible. Her stomach roiled, though there could be no other explanation for his presence at Boston General in the wee hours of the morning. But how had their boss, Jack Wainwright, managed it? Everyone knew Rathe McKay only took exotic assignments overseas. And more important, everyone knew he didn't work with women.

Nia was one of the few who knew why.

Dismay pounded in her temples. She couldn't work with Rathe. He would ruin everything.

"No," she whispered. "This can't be happening."

"My thoughts exactly." Rathe cursed in Russian, his

voice dark and rich like the language. "Was that kick for—" he sucked in a pained breath and straightened slowly "—self-defense, or for what happened before?"

The question jabbed right beneath her heart. She wasn't prepared for this. Wasn't prepared for *him.*

"Before?" Though guilt stung—she wouldn't have kicked him if he'd identified himself as friend rather than foe—she wasn't willing to apologize again. Wasn't willing to be vulnerable to him again. She crossed her arms and stared at the ceiling to buy a steadying moment. For all the times she'd thought about seeing Rathe again, this scenario didn't even come close to what she'd imagined. "Let me see. Would that be *before* when you took my virginity, kicked me out of your hotel room and disappeared without a word…or *before* when my father, *your best friend,* begged you to come visit him on his deathbed and you never showed?"

Eyes dark, Rathe advanced on her, walking gingerly. She stood her ground and lifted her chin so she could glare scalpels at him, though her stomach knotted with nerves and a flare of traitorous warmth. They stared at each other for a heartbeat. Two.

Finally he turned away, muttering, "This is why women shouldn't be allowed in Investigations—they can't separate their personal lives from their professional ones."

And there it was. Rathe McKay's motto: Women Don't Belong in the Field. Period.

Denial howled in Nia's head, in her heart, but she held the emotions in check because, damn it, he was right. This wasn't the time or place to bring up the past. She had a job to do.

And part of that job was proving to her HFH mentor that she was a capable investigator, fully ready to work in the field.

So she found a frosty smile that hopefully showed nothing of her tumultuous emotions. "You're right. I apologize for being unprofessional. What's done is done. Jack Wainwright said he was pairing me with an older, more experienced investigator, so I suppose I should be honored he chose you. You're as old and experienced as they get."

It was a low blow, aimed at what her father had laughingly called Rathe's Methuselah complex. Though only ten years her senior, the HFH superoperative had always acted twice that.

He narrowed his eyes and scowled. "There won't be an investigation. I'm calling Wainwright in the morning and having you reassigned. This is no place for…" He gestured as though the words were unnecessary.

"This is no place for a woman?" Nia clenched her fists at her sides. Though the HFH Head Office didn't discriminate, there were a few old warhorses who did. Rathe, who'd been in the field more than fifteen years already, considered himself one of them.

"This is no place for Tony's daughter!" He grabbed her by the arms and shook her as though she was eighteen years old again and he'd caught her prying into his field notes. "For God's sake, Nadia. You know this isn't what your father wanted for you. What would he say?"

Righteous anger speared through her. "He's dead. The last thing he said on this earth was, 'Where's Rathe?'" And for that she had hated them both.

Emotion darkened his eyes, though she wasn't sure that it was remorse. He spread his hands. "Nadia, for what it's worth, I'm—"

"Don't," she interrupted, not willing to hear the apology, not willing to let him think that a betrayal of such magnitude could be scrubbed away with a few words. "Don't bother. You're right, this isn't the time or the place for personal conversations. We have a job to do."

She turned and stalked toward the freight elevators at the far end of the subbasement.

"Nadia." His voice seemed to caress the word, bringing back memories best left unremembered.

She stopped and glanced back, steeling herself against the sight of him, strong and virile, an image that could have stepped out of her aching, mindless dreams.

Or her nightmares.

"I prefer to be called Nia now. Nadia is a child's name, and I'm not a child anymore." She lifted her chin, daring him to comment. "We have a meeting with the heads of the Transplant Department at 9:00 a.m. sharp— don't be late."

This time she didn't look back, not even when he called her name. They had three hours until the meeting. She'd need every minute of that to prepare herself for the case.

And to armor herself against the disturbing presence of Rathe McKay.

BY NINE THAT MORNING, Rathe was back to walking upright as he stalked through Boston General, but his temper hadn't mellowed much.

It was temper, he assured himself. Temper that had his blood surging through his veins with a tricky tingling sensation. Temper that had him feeling more alive, more engaged than he had in months or maybe longer.

Temper.

What was Wainwright thinking, partnering him with a woman trainee? He didn't work with women. And even if he did, Nadia French was the last girl he'd choose.

Rathe shook his head, annoyed. No, that wasn't right. This was about her being a woman, not about her being Tony's daughter or about a mistake he'd once made in an airport hotel.

His refusal to work with the opposite gender was based on logic and experience. Period. There was nothing personal about it, and nothing personal between him and Nadia.

Sure, his first glimpse of her had been a kick in the gut, a surge of warmth and energy, but that was only basic man-woman biology. His yang approving of her yin. Nothing personal.

Her thick, dark hair was shorter than he remembered. In fact, *she* was shorter than he remembered, as though his mind had decided her scrappy personality couldn't fit inside such a tiny shell. He'd remembered her eyes right, though. Dark brown, swirling with darker promises, they used to look at him with adoration, as though he was the hero he'd once thought himself.

Now they shone with anger. That was personal. And it was unacceptable in a partner.

Already five minutes late for the briefing, Rathe ducked into a windowed alcove and punched his superior's number into his mid-wave cell phone, a high-tech HFH toy certified safe for use in hospitals. When Jack Wainwright answered, Rathe wasted no time with pleasantries. "I want her off the case. Now."

There was a rumble of amusement. Jack had trained Rathe himself, back before a stray bullet had landed the older man behind a desk. There was respect between the two but little reverence. "McKay. I didn't expect to hear from you until at least nine-fifteen. The meeting can't have even started yet."

"It hasn't. I met my *partner* in the laundry room at 2:00 a.m. this morning. She was getting a jump on the case. She doesn't seem to get that investigators never, *ever* go Lone Ranger." It was HFH policy, and might be enough to convince Jack to pull her off the job.

"You were there, too, so don't pretend you give a damn about policy." Jack's shrug carried down the line. "I know you don't work with women, McKay, but it's not like you two are in the middle of a war zone. It's a bit of petty drug trafficking at a well-funded urban hospital. Enjoy it."

Rathe gritted his teeth, knowing the cushy assignment was Jack's way of saying he thought Rathe needed a break from the real action. "She's a liability."

"No, she's not. She's a transplant specialist, she's fearless, and she was requested by name." Jack's voice hardened into a direct order. "Use her. Teach her. This is what the next generation of HFH investigators looks like, McKay. Get used to it."

The phone went dead in Rathe's hand, and he scowled.

Enjoy it. Get used to it. Jack's words replayed in his mind as he jogged up the stairs to the sixth floor, which housed the Transplant Unit.

Fine. They thought he was burned out? He'd show them. He'd make this the fastest, cleanest investigation they'd ever seen. And he'd do it handicapped with a female partner.

He hit the top of the stairs, and an echo of heat reminded him that it wasn't that simple.

His partner was Nadia French. Nia. Tony's daughter.

Rathe had wanted to see his old friend one last time, had ached to apologize, to forgive and be forgiven and to hold Nadia when her father died.

But sometimes a man had to break a promise to keep a promise. And so he had stayed away.

Taking a deep breath, he pushed through the doors into the office of the director of transplant medicine.

"You're late." From her chair on the visitor's side of the lake-size desk, Nia frowned at him. "I've already told Dr. Talbot about the men with the suspicious laundry hamper, and the van with the—"

"I'll take it from here," he interrupted. "Try to remember that I hold seniority on this case."

She rolled her eyes. "Yes, sir, Dr. McKay, sir."

Rathe ignored her and held out a hand to the older of the two men in the room, a distinguished, white-haired gentleman sporting a bow tie and elegant, steel-rimmed glasses. "I'm Rathe McKay."

"It's a pleasure to meet you, Dr. McKay. Your reputation as the medical community's answer to Indiana Jones precedes you." The older man's handshake was firm. "Michael Talbot. And this," the director of transplant gestured to his companion, a handsome, well-groomed man, "is my assistant director, Logan Hart."

The assistant director nodded but didn't offer a hand. In his early thirties, Hart exuded breeding and education from the ends of his professionally sculpted hair to the tips of his tasseled black leather shoes. He looked a far cry from Rathe, who'd gone from the foster-care system straight to a combined undergraduate/medical degree on an HFH scholarship.

And where had that thought come from, Rathe wondered. He was the man he'd become, not the boy he'd been.

Frowning, he took the visitor's chair beside Nia and focused his attention on the men. "My superior has been in direct contact with your administration. I expect you to grant me all of the necessary access and let me run my own investigation. In exchange I'll provide you a written report of my findings once a week. Is that clear?"

There was dead silence in the office as the balance of power shifted neatly into Rathe's hands—which had been his intention. He needed to take control of the situation right away.

When he was in charge, nobody made mistakes. Everyone lived.

But he could feel Nia fuming at his casual dismissal of what she'd seen in the loading area. The aggravation poured off her in waves. He could smell it coming from her skin, like the memory of—

Like the memory of a mistake. A betrayal.

A lost opportunity.

"Gentlemen?" Rathe forced his voice to sound level when it would have—what? Cracked? Faltered? Impossible—he was a grown man. Things like that didn't happen to him. That was for kids such as Nia. "Do we have an agreement?"

Logan Hart, who looked like a kid himself, frowned, but his boss, Talbot, smiled with a glint of respect in his eyes. He held out his hand a second time, this time in affirmation. "We have an agreement, Dr. McKay. We would be fools not to take advantage of your expertise."

In his peripheral vision, Rathe saw Nia curl her lip. Surprisingly, he had to fight a kink of amusement.

But this was no laughing matter. It was an investigation, and if her little stunt down in the subbasement was any indication, she was going to be a hell of a lot of work to baby-sit while he went about his business.

The director leaned back in his chair and steepled his fingers together. "Basically we're stumped. Transplant patients who would've survived a year ago are dying, and there are gaps in our supplies that suggest theft, but nobody's seen anything." He spread his hands. "I brought this to the head administrator's attention, and he called you."

"What sorts of supplies?" Rathe asked.

At the same time Nia said, "Are there connections among the dead patients?"

Logan Hart grinned at her, and a dimple appeared in his cheek. "Good question. They're all rare type."

Rathe shrugged. "If they're rare tissue type, then they probably waited longest for their transplants and had the worst prognoses. You may just be seeing a blip. Let's focus on the supplies to start with. What's been disappearing?"

Nia frowned but didn't argue.

Talbot pushed a bulging envelope across the desk. "There's a list in here, along with your ID badges and supporting information. Jack Wainwright picked your cover stories. I hope you'll find them acceptable."

Rathe could have sworn Talbot was laughing at him but wasn't sure why. He opened the envelope, shook out its contents and glanced at Nia's information before passing it to her. She would be posing as a transplant specialist visiting the hospital to observe Boston General's procedures, and give a short lecture series. Perfect. She wouldn't have to dissemble much to maintain her cover, which was good. She didn't have the experience he did at sliding into new roles. Chameleonlike, he could assume any cover, pass himself off easily as any of a number of people, such as…Rathe glanced at his packet.

"A janitor? You've *got* to be kidding me!"

Nia lifted a hand to stifle a snicker. When Rathe glared at her, she managed to straighten her face before she said, "It's perfect. You're working the night shift, so you'll be able to watch the loading docks and see what comes and goes. So far, that's our best lead…."

She was right, damn it. But Rathe also knew she was thinking that working the day shift, when he was off, would give her time to do some digging on her own. To prove herself.

He knew, because he'd once been like that himself. He'd learned his lesson the hardest way possible, and he'd be damned if he'd let Tony French's daughter find herself in the same situation.

So he nodded. "You're right. Working the night shift will give me plenty of time to help you with your end of things."

She scowled back. "You'll need to sleep sometime, McKay."

"Not necessarily." He scooped their IDs into the envelope. "I don't sleep much." He nodded to the transplant doctors, who were following the exchange with rapt attention. "Gentlemen. I'll be in touch."

Rathe didn't miss the frown Nia directed at him, nor did he miss noticing how Logan Hart held her hand a moment longer than necessary when they shook.

Kids will be kids, Rathe told himself fiercely, and the words echoed in the voice of Nia's father. Though Rathe had shrugged off his experiences as an on-loan medic in the war-torn country where the two had met over a transfusion, the place had marked Tony. Not long after, Tony had retired from the Army to hunker down in the suburbs with his wife and daughter while he waited for the nightmares to fade.

Rathe hoped they had in the end.

Trying to ignore the tug he felt in his gut when Nia laughed at something Logan Hart said, Rathe spun on his heel and left the office. He never should have come back to the States.

At least when he was abroad, it was easier to forget that he'd slept with his best friend's daughter.

He stalked down the hall, away from the woman and the memories. But he didn't go far. He had a feeling she was going to find every possible opportunity to place herself in danger during this assignment.

Hell, it's what he would do in her situation.

EIGHT HOURS LATER, still annoyed that Rathe hadn't waited around after their meeting so they could plan their case and divvy up the responsibilities, Nia stalked to the garage where she'd parked her car. She couldn't wait to get back to the swanky apartment building that had been donated to Boston General for use by visiting scientists and patients' families.

She'd spent the day going over the notes and famil-iarizing herself with the setup. Slick and well orga-nized, Boston General's Transplant Department boasted twenty beds and enough high-tech gadgets to satisfy even Nia—especially since she had designed a few of them herself during her two years in grad school.

"Brilliant," they had called her, when in reality she had simply been bored. Bored by the classwork, by her fellow students, and by the city itself. She had longed for faraway places that could be reached only by overgrown paths, for adventures like the stories her father had told her. Stories with titles like, "The Time Rathe Was Adopted by Cannibals" or "The Time Rathe Saved the Congo."

Those stories had stopped the day she announced to her parents that she wanted to join HFH when she grew up. Come to think of it, so had Rathe's visits, for the most part.

In the damp garage, Nia missed the car door lock and dropped her keys to the pavement beside her silver Jetta. She bent and retrieved them, and was surprised to find her throat tight with the memory.

"I'm sorry, Daddy," she murmured as she unlocked the car and slipped inside its interior, which smelled of leather and hospital disinfectant. "I know this isn't what you wanted for me."

But her father's plans and hers had diverged a long time ago, even before he got sick.

She backed the Jetta out of her hospital parking slot and drove the vehicle out of the garage, shielding her eyes against the reflected glare of headlights in the rearview mirror. "Geez," she muttered over the classic rock on the radio, "I know it gets dark early this time of year, but are the high beams really necessary?"

The headlights followed her out of the garage and down Washington Street, where she merged slowly with the rest of the "rush" hour traffic.

It wasn't until a mile and three lane shifts later that Nia realized the high beams were still just a few cars behind her.

She was being followed.

"Nonsense," she told herself as nerves prickled in her stomach. "The whole apartment building is owned by the hospital. They're simply going the same place you are."

But that didn't stop her left eye from twitching, as it had the night before when she'd seen the two white-coated men pushing a laundry hamper out of the Transplant Department. And it didn't stop her heart from picking up a beat in fear.

She gripped the leather steering wheel tightly as traffic pushed her toward the entrance to the apartment building's parking garage. Should she drive by and see what Mr. High Beams would do? Or should she park and make a run for it?

What would Rathe do in this situation?

"Argh!" She slapped the steering wheel in frustration and turned into the garage. She had purged that silly, teenage question from her head years ago, along with the crush she'd had on her father's dashing friend. Or so she'd thought. But there it was, reminding her of the man she'd loved at twenty-one and hated not long after.

Mr. High Beams didn't follow her into the garage, and Nia felt faintly ashamed for jumping at shadows. A good investigator needed to be tougher than that.

She parked, climbed out of the Jetta, slung her purse and soft-sided briefcase over her shoulder and tried to stop herself from hurrying to the elevators.

A voice spoke out of the shadows. "We need to talk."

Chapter Two

Nia gasped and jolted, though the quick thunder of her heart identified Rathe before he stepped out into the light. She took an involuntary step back, snagged her foot on a crack and stumbled.

He caught her before she fell, one strong hand grabbing her arm, the other curving around her waist and sending a lightning bolt of sensation through her chest.

"Let me go!" She struggled to get away, not from him, but from the effect he had on her.

He released her quickly, though kept a hand up to make sure she was steady. A shadow moved across his face. "You needn't be afraid of me, Nadia."

Nadia.

It was the name her father had given her, the name he'd called her until the day he died. The memory of it brought a phantom ache to the scar beside her navel, and the threat of tears to her eyes. She pressed her fingers to her temples, where the first tendrils of a headache had gathered. It was late, that was all. She wasn't usually this vulnerable to memories.

"Go away, Rathe." Her quiet voice held the accumulated stress of the day.

Of all the times she'd imagined their reunion…

"We have things to discuss." He stood between her and the elevator, though she sensed he wouldn't stop her from boarding. No, he would just ride up with her, which could not be allowed. He'd had his chance to be a part of her life, a part of her family, and he'd turned it down without even a reply, just a packet of letters marked Return To Sender.

She shook her head, feeling the echoes of old sorrow, newer frustration. This would never work. There was no way she and Rathe could function together as a team. "We could've talked anytime today, you didn't need to follow me home. Right now I'm tired and I have a full day of surgery to observe tomorrow, so I'm going to bed. We'll talk in the morning."

She moved to brush past him, but he caught her arm and waited until she looked up at him. "Nadia. Nia. I didn't follow you. Talbot told me where you were billeted, so I waited here for you." He paused a beat. "Why? Did someone follow you?" When she didn't answer right away, he shook her. "Nia! *Were you followed?*"

She thought of the high beams behind her, the feeling of creeping malevolence they'd given her and the relief she'd felt when she turned into the garage and they moved on by. "No, of course not."

"You always were a lousy liar. Damn it! This is all because of that crazy stunt you pulled in the laundry area." Looking suddenly tired, he released her arm, stepped forward and stabbed the elevator call button. "Come on. We need to set some ground rules. If you keep this up you'll get yourself killed."

"Why are you being like this?" Nia's voice rose as her frustration moved to the fore. She was tired and confused, and though his presence complicated everything, she wasn't going to bow out of her first official investigation simply because he wanted her to. "Why are you set on running me off this case? Is it *personal?* Is it because we were lovers? If so—" she dredged up the words she'd said so many times in the fantasies where he'd come back and begged for another chance "—you're the one who walked, McKay, not me."

Technically he hadn't walked; he'd sent her back to her father. Somehow that had been worse.

"This has nothing to do with ancient history," he snapped, though Nia swore that, for a moment, his eyes dropped to where her snazzy leather jacket hung over her breasts. Heat climbed her cheeks as he continued, "Nothing!"

"Then what *is* it about?"

He paused for a moment, seeming to struggle with the answer. Then he exhaled noisily. "You're a woman, Nia, and I don't work with women. You know that."

It was one of the stories her father hadn't told her, one she'd overheard her parents discussing late at night. Rathe's partner, Maria, had been killed while they were on assignment. Not long after the incident, he had come to live with Nadia's family for a few weeks. Gaunt and sad-eyed, he hadn't spoken much. He'd spent most of his time sitting down by the beach with an empty sketchpad on his knee.

At eighteen, Nadia had known him only from her father's stories. Though Tony had told her to leave Rathe alone, she had found excuses to wander down by the water. She'd sat on the steps above him, each day bringing a different book, until he'd finally turned around and asked, "What are you reading?"

She'd blushed and shown him the cover of a travel book about Bateo, wishing it were something more sophisticated. A text from her advanced P-chem class maybe, or a mature story about unrequited love.

"I've been there, you know," he'd said.

And though she knew he'd been to Bateo—from the story entitled "The Time Rathe Stopped an Outbreak of Blood Fever"—she had shaken her head and asked him to tell her about the island. He'd described the way the light slanted down between the leaves high above, and how the bugs were bigger, the animals meaner, and the natives tougher than any she'd see in the States.

As he'd talked, his eyes had glowed a molten silver, his shoulders had squared and his back had straightened until he looked like the man she'd expected to meet, not the sad, hollow figure who'd sat down by the beach and sketched nothing.

The next morning he was gone. Inside her heavy book bag—she'd been in her third year of college by then—she'd found a sheet of paper folded inside the book on Bateo. On it was a pencil drawing of a jungle scene with some of the prettiest leaves, biggest bugs, and meanest-eyed creatures she could imagine.

After that he'd sent her presents once or twice—a colorful feather arrangement and a cowrie shell necklace she'd kept in a carved box beside her bed. Then he'd come back the year she turned twenty-one, and everything had changed.

And changed again.

Now she angled her chin up at him. "Yes, I'm a woman, but I'm also damn good at my job. Just ask Wainwright." She knew full well Rathe had already called their boss, just as she knew he'd pushed to have her yanked from the case and been turned down. "Even better, open your eyes and see for yourself."

"It's not that." He pinched the bridge of his nose.

"Yes, it is." She stepped into the empty elevator car, bracing an arm across the opening to keep him out. "And for your information, I'm not quitting. If you can't work with me, you'll have to take yourself off the case."

A large part of her hoped he would do just that. A smaller, more feminine part hoped he wouldn't.

He scowled. "Damn it, Nia! Let me come up. We need to talk about this." The air around him vibrated with tension, and his eyes seemed to shoot silver sparks, but she wasn't afraid of him.

Not physically, at least.

She stepped back and pulled her finger off the open-door button. "No. We'll talk about it tomorrow. Meet me in the coffee shop at seven."

The doors tried to slide shut. He blocked them with

his shoulder and glared at her. "Fine. But promise me one thing. Promise you won't snoop around the hospital again tonight. Leave that to me, okay?"

Nia might have taken offense at the request, but she was too darned tired to do more than collapse into bed. And there was something in his frustration, in his suddenly human gaze, that told her the request wasn't just the primary asking his junior investigator not to interfere.

Her father might have called it "The Time Rathe Asked for a Favor."

Confused, stirred up and weary beyond words, she simply nodded. "Fine. I won't go back to the hospital tonight. I'll see you in the morning."

A glint that might have been relief, might have been triumph, flashed in his eyes and he let go of the elevator doors. "Tomorrow, then." He turned and walked away as the panels slid shut.

This time it was Nia who slapped a hand to keep them open. "Rathe!" He stopped and looked back without turning. She felt suddenly foolish, but something compelled her to call, "Be careful."

Maybe he smiled. Maybe he winced. But after holding her eyes with his for a heartbeat, Rathe simply inclined his head and turned away.

Nia let the doors slide shut and resisted the urge to press her suddenly hot face against the cool metal wall.

THE NEXT MORNING Rathe leaned back in an uncomfortable booth and watched Nia enter the hospital coffee shop. A restless night was etched in the deep circles under her eyes. Her skin was tinted with makeup, but the hollows remained. And, damn it, they didn't detract one iota from her beauty.

Her dark hair curled around her face, adding mysterious shadows to eyes that already knew him too well. A faint blush stained her high cheeks, and her full, sensuous lips drew into a flat line as she sank down opposite him, both hands wrapped around a cup of coffee. She grinned at him, though the expression didn't quite reach her eyes. "Okay, Bwana. Teach me how to investigate."

Rathe frowned but didn't argue. During the long night, he'd acknowledged he would have to teach her some basic survival skills, since she seemed determined to see this through. He would walk her through a safely edited version of an in-hospital covert job, and try like hell to convince her it wasn't what she wanted to do with her life. He just couldn't picture her in the Investigations Division, all five-foot-something of her pitted against the ugliness that lurked beneath the underbelly of the medical community.

Why? He wanted to ask. *Why are you so set on investigations? Your father would've hated it. You could be hurt. Killed. Why?*

But that was personal, not business. So instead he pushed a sheet of paper across the table to her. "Let's start with the laundry room. Why did you follow those men out to the loading dock?"

"What's this?" She picked up the paper, scanned its contents and answered her own question, "It's the pickup timetable for the linens. There was a team scheduled for the one-to-three shift the other morning." She glanced up at him. "Why wasn't this information in our background packets?"

Rathe shrugged. "Who knows? I copied it from the schedule in the maintenance office..." among other things that she didn't need to know about. He would tell her enough to do her part of the job and no more. He'd pass along enough to satisfy her, plus a little disinformation to keep her away from the dangerous parts.

Though the case seemed simple on the surface, Rathe had a feeling it was anything but.

"So how do you explain the bed and all the equipment we saw in that so-called laundry van?"

"I didn't see it." When she raised an eyebrow, he shrugged. "I didn't get there until after the door was shut."

There was no need to tell her that he'd been nearly panic-stricken to see the tiny, furtive figure of a woman heading for the departing van. In an instant he'd been back in the Tehruvian jungle, seeing Maria wave from a rebel army transport.

And that was *before* he'd realized the shadow in the laundry room belonged to Nadia French.

"Why were you there, anyway? We weren't supposed to start work until later that morning." She pursed her lips and blew across the top of her coffee. Sipped. Swallowed.

Rathe looked away. He had to keep this professional. Mentor and student. Senior and junior. The way it should have been from the very first day he'd noticed his best friend's daughter watching him from the beachfront stairs.

"I was looking around," he replied, not mentioning the gut feeling that had drawn him down to the subbasement. He tapped the paper that now lay on the table between them. "Unless you have a compelling reason why you followed those two, I think we should move on." Rather, she should move on and leave the subbasement to him.

"You're going to disregard what I saw in the van?" Her fingers tightened enough to dent the cardboard cup.

"No." Rathe shook his head. "Not disregard. File and continue." He held up a finger. "Rule one—Don't fall in love with your own theory. When that happens, you'll overlook clues that don't fit."

He waited for the argument, but she surprised him by nodding. She sipped, then gestured to encompass the hospital. "It's like making a diagnosis. Don't pick a disease until you've gathered all the facts."

"Right. Only, think of the entire hospital, or maybe the Transplant Department, as the patient. As a doctor, you're already used to that sort of investigation. This is simply on a grander scale." A more dangerous one, though he was determined not to let her experience that firsthand. In the wee hours of the morning, when he'd tried to catnap in the basement break room, he'd decided on that course, with one addition: he was going to do his damnedest to convince her that HFH in general—and investigations in particular—wasn't for her.

It was what Tony would've wanted him to do.

"So our symptoms are as follows," she began, ticking the points off on her fingers. "First, there's an increase in transplant deaths. Second, supply shortages are reported to Transplant Director Talbot and Assistant Director Hart."

Rathe thought she might have lingered on the second man's name and he scowled. That was another thing about working with women. They couldn't keep their minds on business.

She blew on her coffee again, and Rathe forced himself to glance around the near-empty café. They weren't being overheard. And he was a hypocrite, watching her make love to a cardboard cup while he preached to himself about women and their inability to focus on the job.

He gritted his teeth and gestured for her to continue.

"They're missing antirejection drugs. Suture kits. That sort of thing." Another finger joined the first two. "And third, I saw two men leave Transplant with a full laundry cart, even though the linens hadn't been changed out. They loaded the cart into a van rigged with life support and then…" She glared at him. "Thanks to you, I don't know what happened to the hamper from there."

Annoyed, Rathe fired back, "Thanks to me, you didn't break your neck trying some damn fool stunt in an attempt to—" He stopped himself. "Never mind. We've already covered that and you promised not to go down there again without me." He fixed her with a look. "Right?"

"Sure. Whatever." She glanced at her watch. "I'm scheduled to observe a rare-type kidney transplant in a little less than an hour. If we're done here, I'm going up to my office to read over the rest of the material Talbot left for me."

Done? They hadn't even started yet, but Rathe didn't argue the point. It was probably a good thing their covers would keep them separated for the most part. At night he could investigate the depths of the hospital, where he was positive the real machinations were occurring. During the day, he could keep watch over her and make sure she didn't get too close to the danger he could feel fermenting below the surface of this case.

And sleep? He'd never needed much of that. Like Tony had always said, *I'll sleep plenty when I'm dead.*

"Dream well, old friend," Rathe murmured to himself, forgetting for the moment that Tony's daughter sat opposite him.

"What was that?"

Rathe shook his head. "Nothing." He stood. "We'll meet after the transplant, compare notes and divvy up which one of us will follow which line of inquiry. That'll save us from duplicating efforts." And allow him to keep her on the outskirts of the heavy lifting.

"Fine." She tipped her head, considering. "But we shouldn't meet in public again. It would look strange, don't you think?"

Irritated that he hadn't thought of that first, which just went to show that mixed-sex partnerships were needlessly distracting, Rathe scowled. "You're right. There's no reason for a visiting lecturer to socialize with a janitor." He tried not to let their respective roles annoy him, but Jack Wainwright had no doubt laughed long and loud when he'd decided on their cover stories.

Rathe McKay, legend-turned-janitor.

Oh, well. That made it a hell of a cover.

"We could meet in my office this afternoon," she suggested tongue in cheek. "You could bring your mop and pretend—"

"I got it," he growled, trying not to see the absurd humor in it. "But your office won't work every day— it'll look suspicious. Why don't we meet at your apartment at change of shift, instead?"

"No. Absolutely not." She tipped her chin down, eyes suddenly dark.

Rathe shrugged, trying not to care. "Fine. We'll figure it out later. You go do your thing, Doc. I'll be around."

He watched her walk away and saw a hint of the young woman who'd once sat down beside him on the beach and showed him a book about Bateo. Like that teenager, Nia was still unsatisfied with who she was, where she was, always looking for the next thing that was just out of reach.

They were, Rathe acknowledged with a wry grimace, entirely too alike.

He swept her empty coffee cup off the table and crumpled it in one hand as he hesitated at the café door. He could return to the warren of corridors and small rooms in the basement that were the realm of the maintenance workers, the laundry crews and the other tradespeople who came and went through the large hospital. Rife with gossip and the occasional scoundrel, that was where he'd find the information he sought. He was sure of it.

He glanced over at the big bank of brushed-steel elevator doors that would carry him up into the ivory towers, to the wide, straight corridors and large airy rooms of the treatment and research floors where Nia belonged.

He muttered a curse and turned his back on the temptation. She would have to keep herself out of trouble for an hour. She could do it. She was a big girl now.

Or so she kept insisting.

OVER THE NEXT HOUR, Nia couldn't cobble the information into a decent theory no matter how hard she tried. The failure grated on her as she shut and locked her office and headed down to the café. She barely had time to grab a quick snack before she observed Dr. Talbot transplant a healthy donor kidney into a young woman who had been born with small, subfunctional organs.

Nia rubbed at the faint scar above her hipbone while she waited for the elevator, her mind still on the mystery she was supposed to be unraveling. She had plenty of questions, but her theories were anemic at best.

The missing supplies made some sense—almost any medical item could be sold on the black market. And it was possible, if not likely, that the laundry hamper was being used to transport the pharmaceuticals down to the loading dock and out of the hospital. That would assume at least one thief had access to the locked supplies. Short Whiny Guy and Cadaver Man were her first guesses. Surely she and Rathe could find the pair.

Rathe. No, she refused to think about him. They had agreed to leave the past where it belonged. He hadn't wanted the family that had loved him as a son, and he hadn't wanted the woman who had loved him as a man. In the seven years since she'd last seen him, she had outgrown both her love and her desire to follow in his footsteps across the globe and back.

She'd decided to blaze her own trail instead.

"Focus," she told herself sternly, glad she was alone in the descending elevator. "This isn't about you or Rathe. It's about the patients and the hospital."

But none of this added up. How did the missing supplies account for the increase in transplant deaths? Were the two even related?

The doors slid open, and Nia stepped out into the big, open atrium at the center of the hospital, where all the wings intersected. A flash of navy blue caught her eye and she glanced over, half expecting to see Rathe waiting for her, ready to tell her where she could go, who she could see and what she could do.

But it was someone else, a stoop-shouldered old man in a janitor's dark-blue uniform, listlessly swabbing at a puddle of something she didn't care to know about.

Ignoring the single twitch of that restless muscle at the corner of her eye, Nia hurried to the café and bought a muffin to make up for the breakfast she'd been too keyed up to eat. She reversed direction and headed back to the elevators, biting into the muffin as her stomach growled.

A heavy blow from behind drove her to her knees.

"Gonna getcha, bitch!" The high-pitched, almost giggling voice near her ear lodged quick panic in her throat.

She hit the floor, the muffin bounced away, and her left eye nearly locked itself shut. Her attacker followed her down and lay crosswise atop her.

Nia squirmed desperately and tried to scream, but the huge, smothering weight drove the breath from her lungs. Faintly she heard cries of alarm. Running feet.

Her heart hammered in her ears, and terror sweated from her palms. Every self-defense move she'd learned was useless. She had no leverage. She pushed against the floor, but to no avail.

"Where's your money? Where is it?" Rough hands groped at her pockets, at her body. She fought back, jabbing with her feet and elbows whenever her attacker's weight shifted enough to allow it. But her blows sank into heavy, hot blubber and she still couldn't breathe.

"Where is it?" The man flipped her over, looming large in her oxygen-starved vision. His face was pocked with scars, some from acne, some from injuries. His hair was greasy and limp, his face covered with rank sweat. "Where is your money?"

She didn't need to see the needle tracks on his upraised arm to know he was beyond reason. He raised his arm higher, and a switchblade glittered in a ray of sunlight.

Running feet thundered. A woman screamed.

And the knife descended in a killing arc.

Chapter Three

Time seemed to slow, picking out Nia's last few moments in exquisite detail. She saw the distended, bulging veins in her attacker's forearm, saw an onlooker's mouth form a perfect *O* of horror. She smelled sour, unwashed man and the sharp taint of her own fear. She felt the weight of him, like that of a lover, pressing her into the hard floor, shifting atop her as the blade descended.

And she wished, with a burning intensity that was close to pain, that she had been a better daughter.

Then the knife completed its arc and the world sped up again. Navy blue flashed before Nia's eyes. Her attacker jolted and fell to the side. The switchblade hit the polished marble, chimed like a bell and skipped harmlessly away.

Free! She was free!

Not stopping to question it, she scrambled to a crouch, ready to escape if possible, fight if necessary. But she didn't need to do either. Her attacker's attention had shifted to the old, stoop-shouldered maintenance man who'd come to her rescue.

Only it wasn't an old janitor.

Navy ball cap missing, and a broken-off mop handle in his hands, Rathe faced the bear-size junkie, who swayed on his feet and shook his head as though to clear it. But the rheumy eyes were disconcertingly sharp as they focused with deadly intent.

"You got money? I need a fix, man. Just gimme a fix and I'll go away. I don't want to hurt you, man." The drug-crazed giant belied this by taking a swipe at Rathe, who darted out of reach.

"McKay, look out!" Nia cried, then belatedly remembered their cover. She wasn't supposed to know him.

His eyes flicked to her, and the junkie charged with a roar, nearly catching the "janitor" by surprise.

Rathe stepped back and spun the mop handle in a neat one-two-three tattoo that caught the man on the ribs, throat and just behind the ear. Seemingly undeterred, the attacker lurched forward, hamlike arms reaching. But his drug-induced invincibility propelled him straight into a whistling arc of wood as Rathe teed off on his attacker's temple. And this time, he put some muscle into it. The mop handle met flesh with a thud and a crack as the beleaguered wood broke under pressure. The enormous man dropped like a rock.

And stayed down.

Nobody moved for a beat, then scattered applause broke out in the atrium. Voices murmured. Gentle, helping hands tugged at Nia, pulling her to her feet and checking her for injury. But the voices seemed muted, the touches faraway. Her whole attention was centered on the man who stood above his fallen enemy, making the navy janitor's garb look like a warrior's armor.

"Rathe," she whispered, and though he was twenty feet away, his head snapped up. His eyes found hers, and the energy surged between them as it had once before, hot and wanting, sharp and ready. Then, like a suddenly stilled heart, the connection was broken as he looked away. His shoulders sagged. He seemed to shrink. His eyes dulled to those of a bored laborer whose mind was on other things. He bent and retrieved his ball cap, looking more washed out than he'd been seven years earlier, near dead with fever.

He'd been holed up in an airport hotel, having landed near collapse and been unable to make it further. Twenty-one-year-old Nadia, halfway through her accelerated M.D., had gotten the message before her father. This was it, she'd thought. This was her way of proving to her father that she was cut out for HFH. Her way of proving to Rathe that she was worthy of—

"Ma'am? Excuse me, ma'am? The officers are here. Ma'am? Are you okay?" The gentle hands shook her out of the past and back to a present that included a mess of hospital security guards, an unconscious junkie and a switchblade lying, seemingly harmless, on the floor.

Eyes fixed on the knife, Nia began to shake.

Over the roaring in her ears, she heard someone say, "Hey, grab her, she's going to faint!" just as another voice, farther away, asked, "Where'd that janitor go? He was here a minute ago."

Rathe. The name steadied her, reminded her she was

alive, thanks to him. Reminded her that she had a job to do. The reputation of her sex to uphold. She could imagine him scoffing at her. *This is why women shouldn't be in dangerous field situations. They fall apart.*

Well, damn it. Not her. Not today.

"I'm fine." She batted away the helping hands and turned toward the knot of security guards, who gave way to a pair of men in street clothes.

The younger of the two, handsome in a neat brown suit and crisp white shirt, held out his hand. "Detective Peters, ma'am." He indicated his partner with his other hand, and a wedding band glinted gold in the light. For some reason Nia found the symbol comforting. "And my partner, Detective Sturgeon. We were in the neighborhood."

The older detective, long-jowled and smelling faintly of peppermints, nodded gravely. "Ma'am. What can you tell us about the incident?"

"He said he wanted my money," she answered, scrambling to put the kaleidoscopic memories of the last few minutes into some sort of order. "He had needle marks on his arms and his eyes…" She trailed off, realizing something for the first time.

His eyes had been normal. Calculating. And murderous.

HALF AN HOUR LATER, Nia fumbled to unlock her office door with shaking hands. She'd answered the detectives' questions and arranged for them to meet with Talbot and Hart. She'd watched the pockmarked man wake up cursing, and had seen him stagger off between a pair of uniformed officers, still cursing. She'd assured the onlookers she was fine, and professed ignorance at what had become of the janitor.

All in all, she thought she'd held it together well. But now she was in her office, alone. It was okay to fall apart.

She closed the door behind her and didn't turn on the lights as she slumped against the wall and felt the switch poke into her spine. She pressed the back of her hand to her lips and willed the tears to come.

But there were no tears. In their place was a nagging sense of guilt that she'd realized something important in those last few moments, and it had been just as quickly forgotten. Overlapping that was an edgy energy that seemed to curl red and blue behind her closed eyelids.

After a few moments the shakes subsided, and Nia realized that whatever stubborn streak had forced her to defy her father's wishes and go off into the unknown... that part of her wouldn't let the tears come now.

"Damn it." She pushed away from the door, slapped on the light and froze when she saw the man sitting in the chair behind her borrowed desk.

"My sentiments exactly," Rathe concurred. His eyes gleamed with an indefinable emotion that sent skitters of heat racing through her body. His cap lay on the desk. The dark blue coveralls were open several buttons at the throat and rolled up at the sleeve to expose the corded muscles beneath the tanned skin of his forearms. His shoulders were square and powerful, and with a start, Nia realized he could turn the uniform from a disguise to a fashion statement with a simple change in posture and expression.

He stood, uncoiling slowly from the chair as though afraid she might bolt. But bolting was the last thing on her mind as she identified the heady, racing sensation that had pounded through her during the fight and set her hands to shaking afterward. Excitement. This was it. This was the adventure she craved, the thrill she'd been seeking.

This was it.

She wasn't sure why it had been lacking in her previous assignments, or why she'd found it in an urban hospital rather than in the midst of a deep, dark forest, but there it was. The adrenaline poured through her body, throbbed at her nerve endings and clamored in her head. She wanted to run. She wanted to dance, to sing, to tip her head back and scream.

Wanting to include him in her joy, she grinned at Rathe.

His eyes narrowing, he advanced on her and leaned down so they were face-to-face. "This is not a joke, Nia. I expected better of you!" Stunned, she drew back, but he followed, crowding her against the closed door with his body and his anger. "Don't you get it? You could've been killed out there." He stabbed a finger towards the atrium, then placed his palm flat against the door beside her head, effectively trapping her.

"Well, I wasn't, thanks to you," she fired back. "That's why HFH doctors work in teams, remember? So we can watch each other's backs." She shoved at his chest with both hands, but he was like sun-warmed granite, hard and immovable. "Damn it, let me go!"

She saw the change in his eyes, a flash of resignation and a wash of heat. Her body answered the call before she was even aware of receiving it, and he bent close and whispered, "I can't."

Then he kissed her, and all that restless, edgy energy redirected itself to her lips, and to the places where their bodies merged. Her palms burned where they rested on his coveralls. Almost without volition, her fingers curved into the material and held fast.

The gap of seven years was bridged in that first instant of contact. Her lips parted on a sigh as they were covered with his, the touch surprisingly gentle for such a hard, elemental man.

She dug her fingers in deeper, feeling the wall of his chest beneath the coarse coverall material. Unsatisfied, she slid one hand up, into the vee of his unbuttoned uniform, and found warm, resilient flesh covered with a smattering of hair.

Warm flesh, not hot. He'd been hot before, burning with fever and smelling faintly of exotic spices and sickness. The memory seared her with excitement and a dull undercurrent of shame.

"Nia." He broke the kiss for a moment to search her eyes. "I'm sorry. I shouldn't have done that, but that scene in the atrium scared the hell out of me." He pressed his lips to her temple, like he'd done the morning he'd sent her back to her father. "Please. If you've ever forgiven what I did to you, to your father, please give me this. Please pull out of Investigations and find something safer to do."

His tone, and the casual caress, stabbed straight into her heart, which she'd long ago tried to armor against the memory of Rathe McKay. But his words brought a wash of pure, clean anger to chase away the thrill of his touch. "Something safer?" She cursed in Arabic and had the satisfaction of seeing him wince. "What is your definition of *safe?* Should I spend the rest of my days barefoot, pregnant and waiting for my man to come home?"

He let her go and stalked away, stopping on the opposite side of the desk. "No, of course not." He stared at a generic poster of a cheerful-looking palm tree shading an empty beach. "But this isn't what your father wanted for you. He didn't want you working dangerous assignments for HFH, and he didn't want you involved with—" He broke off and cursed. "He didn't want you involved with any of this."

The pain pulsed in her heart and low in her back. "Don't you *dare* speak of my father. You have no right."

He grimaced. "Think what you will, but Tony was the best friend I ever had. Yours was the closest thing I ever had to a family."

"Yet you abandoned us," Nia said quietly, hating that her voice broke when she said, "You abandoned *me.* My father."

"I did what I thought was best."

"You did what came naturally." She turned away, betrayal and need tangling together in a messy ball in her chest. "You ignored the people who loved you. Just like in Tehru."

There was a beat of silence. Another. The room chilled.

Nia couldn't believe she'd said that. Couldn't believe she'd even thought it. Her anger fled from a wash of shame, and she stretched out a hand. "Rathe, I'm sorry. I didn't mean—"

He stepped away, eyes blank. "Sure you did. And you're right, at least about what happened with Maria. Which proves my point. Women don't belong in war zones. They don't belong in dangerous situations. And they sure as hell shouldn't traipse around the world looking for trouble." He scowled and looked away. "Quit HFH while you can, Nadia. Start a medical practice somewhere safe. Pediatrics in a small town, maybe, or a GP near your mother. You're not cut out for this life."

She hissed through her teeth. "Because I'm a woman?"

He nodded shortly. "This isn't going to work. I can't mentor you if I have to keep saving you from jumping on the back of a moving laundry van or being knifed in the damn lobby." He reached for the doorknob, opened the door he'd pressed her against minutes earlier while they kissed. "I'll call Jack and ask him to reassign you. After what just happened, I'm sure he'll agree it's for the best. You're simply not tough enough for Investigations."

She lifted her chin. "You have no idea how tough I am, McKay. Don't think you know me because you knew my father."

"I know enough," he said flatly, still not meeting her eyes.

"Fine," she snapped. "But don't bother calling Wainwright. I'll do it." She turned her back, lifted the phone and waited pointedly for him to leave. When she heard the door close behind him, she lowered the handset and pressed both hands flat to the desk as the fight drained out of her.

This assignment wasn't anything like she'd imagined it would be.

She'd had it all planned out, how she'd impress the senior investigator with her quick wits and—if necessary—her guts. How they would solve the case in record time and shock Wainwright.

And if news of her success reached Rathe McKay in some far-off land, she'd imagined he might be happy for her. A little proud. And maybe, just maybe, he would think of her and regret dismissing her twice—once when he'd pushed her from his bed and again later when he'd brusquely refused to see Tony that last time.

But nothing about this job had turned out right. Nothing.

Nia sighed and picked up the phone. She stabbed Wainwright's number and waited while his secretary put her through.

He sounded concerned. She'd never called him during an assignment before. "Nia? What's wrong? Do you have a problem?"

She tightened her fingers on the receiver and wished there was another way. "No, Jack. *You* have a problem."

IN A SERVICE ELEVATOR headed down to the depths of Boston General, Rathe rubbed his chest where the skin felt tight and tender. An odd sensation flooded through him. It was shame, perhaps, and disappointment that Nia had agreed to be reassigned. It surprised him that she'd given in so easily.

Don't think you know me, she'd said, but he knew enough. He knew that she had grown into a beautiful woman—a beautiful *younger* woman, though the ten years between them didn't seem as important now as they had before. And he knew that the kiss they'd shared upstairs would haunt him once she was gone, just as the memory of her touch had stayed with him long after he'd hopped on an airplane to wherever, with the imprint of Tony's fist tattooed on his jaw.

The elevator doors opened and Rathe stepped out, remembering that day and the pain. The subbasement echoed with a noisy quiet, filled with hisses of steam and the hum of machinery nearly below the level of his hearing. Above the background he heard a whisper of sound. A cough or perhaps a footstep.

He tensed. The skin on the back of his neck tightened, though there was no logical reason for it. Any number of hospital personnel could be in the subbasement for legitimate reasons.

But his instincts told him otherwise.

With a flash of gratitude that Nia was safe upstairs and soon to be assigned to another HFH division, he eased closer to the puke-green cinder block wall and crept toward the corner up ahead, where a second corridor branched off the main hallway. The noise came again, and this time there was no mistaking it. Running footsteps.

"Damn!" Discarding stealth for speed, Rathe sprinted

around the corner. Ahead, a tall, navy-clad figure disappeared around the next bend.

Flight doesn't always equal guilt, the HFH manuals warned. Maybe that was true elsewhere in the world, but not at Boston General. He'd bet his medical degree that this guy was running for a reason.

Well, he wouldn't get far. Rathe ducked his head and accelerated, glad that he'd traded the janitor's standard sneakers for his own custom-made boots, which were tough enough to protect him from desert sands and soft enough to render him nearly silent. Doors sped past, and he skidded a little when he turned the corner and stopped dead.

The loading dock. Damn. The door swung shut on a slice of the outdoors, leaving the dimly lit area empty. "Bloody hell," he said aloud and reached for the door.

The attack hit him from behind. A man grabbed him and shoved him into the wall. Hard.

Rathe reacted instantly, jabbing an elbow back and twining his foot around the other man's ankle, but his assailant was taller and light on his feet. The bigger man spun away. His elbow cracked against Rathe's jaw. Rathe's head whipped to the side, and he swung out blindly, felt a spurt of satisfaction when he connected and heard a grunt of pain.

He yanked off his ball cap for better visibility and sent his fist into the gaunt, gray face of his attacker. Dimly he recognized Cadaver Man from Nia's description, and the realization that the bastard could have hurt her lent fury to his blows.

He wound up for the knockout when the cell phone hidden inside his coveralls rang. The noise distracted him for only an instant, but it was long enough for the gray, corpselike man to slip inside his guard and punch him in the gut. Rathe doubled over, then dropped to the floor, rolling away in case there was a follow-up kick. But there wasn't. The tall man stared down at him for a heartbeat, a disconcerting lack of expression on his face.

After five rings, the cell phone fell silent.

"Go away, Dr. McKay," Cadaver Man said in an unexpectedly soft voice laced with the cadences of northern Maine, "and call off Nia French. Or else."

And he shouldered his way through the door and out into the bustling streets of Chinatown.

Rathe lurched to his feet, thinking to give chase even though he knew it was no use. Then the cell phone rang again, and a name leaped to lightning-sharp focus in his mind. *Nia!*

The bastard knew their names and their purpose. What if he'd already gotten to her?

He slapped the phone open. "Nia? Are you okay?"

"McKay. What the hell are you doing?" The booming voice on the other end of the line was familiar, though it certainly wasn't Nia.

"Jack," Rathe held the phone to his ear and jogged back the way he'd come. "I'm glad it's you. We have a problem."

The elevator was slow in coming and he waited impatiently, telling himself she was fine. She was in her office. Safe. This was Boston, not Tehru, damn it.

Wainwright's voice was sharp. "You're damn right we have a problem. Nia French says you told her to quit."

Rathe stepped into the elevator and stabbed a button. Forced himself to breathe evenly. She was fine. He was overreacting. He wasn't going to let this happen again. "Yes, I did. There's something going on in this hospital. Something bad. I want her out of here before she gets herself hurt."

"You're ditching the assignment?"

Rathe scowled into the phone. "Of course not. You know better than that, Jack. I'm staying, but I want Nia out of danger." The service elevator let him off in the lobby, and he transferred to one of the brushed-steel lifts that would carry him up to the Transplant Department.

Wainwright's grumble vibrated on the airwaves. "It's her job to be in danger, McKay. Remember?"

"Doesn't matter," Rathe retorted. "She quit."

"No. She didn't quit. She phoned me and threatened to sue both our asses for sexual discrimination."

"She did *what?*" Rathe ignored the curious stares of the two white-coated researchers sharing the car with him. He supposed the image was incongruous—a rumpled janitor shouting into a phone boasting technology that hadn't yet transitioned from the military to the public.

"You heard me." Wainwright's voice dropped to a threatening hiss. "Fix this, McKay. I don't care how you do it, but fix this. She's one of the best young M.D.s I've got. I will *not* lose her, do you understand?"

The doors slid open and Rathe stepped out of the car. He glanced around to make sure he was alone, then lowered his voice and grated, "She'll be lost for good if you don't pull her off this case, get it? I just tangled with one of our suspects and he called me by name. Worse, he knew her name, too."

There was a beat of silence. Then Jack sighed. "Proceed with caution, McKay. That's all we can ever do in these situations." He paused. "You're in contact with the local police?"

Rathe gripped the phone so tightly his knuckles cracked. "Damn it! Haven't you heard a word I've said? Nia is in danger, and I want her off the case. Now."

"This isn't your call, McKay. I don't want a harassment suit on my hands, and more important, I want Nia French in Investigations. She's a brilliant doctor and she has no fear. I want you to train her, Rathe, not protect her." There was a heavy silence. "If you can't handle it, then I'll pull you off the case and give her to someone who can. Jacobsen is free right now, or maybe Roscoe."

Rathe cursed in Russian, his favorite language for profanity. "Jacobsen is practically a rookie himself, and Roscoe is—" too jaded, too handsome, too slick with the ladies and just a little bit careless "—not right for this case." He lowered his voice further as a group of med students filed by in the wake of Director Talbot, who frowned as though wondering why his undercover operative was skulking near the elevator. "Please, Jack. Take her off this case. I'll train her on another job, I swear it. Just not this one. I've got a bad feeling."

Wainwright's voice gentled, as though he knew something about the things Rathe preferred to keep hidden. "She'll be fine. She's smart and she's tough. Just watch her back. That's all partners can ever ask of each other." And the line went dead.

"Damn it!" Rathe jammed the phone back inside his coveralls and strode to Nia's borrowed office. "You'd better be at your desk, Nia French," he muttered. "You'd better be okay, because if you're not…"

Just watch her back, Jack had said. Well, Rathe hadn't been watching just now. Not well enough.

He slammed through her door, which hung slightly ajar, and froze. Tension boiled like bile in his stomach.

She wasn't there. And the office was a wreck.

Chapter Four

Emergency!

The call crackled over the intercom, and the hallway was suddenly filled with the noise of running feet as nurses and doctors rushed to answer the call.

In a supply closet nearby, Nia heard the commotion and felt her eyelid twitch. She shoved a box of syringes back onto its shelf, jammed the inventory list into her pocket and slipped into the corridor, hoping her tic was wrong.

She wanted a break in the case, yes, but not at the expense of a patient.

"Marissa! I told you to call me if she deteriorated!" Logan Hart shouldered Nia aside without apology and pushed his way through a knot of scrub-clad nurses into the patient's room.

"I'm sorry, Dr. Hart. It happened so quickly, I didn't—" The dark-haired nurse trailed off when she realized the handsome young doctor wasn't listening. She made a face and turned away, then frowned when she saw Nia had witnessed the break in protocol. Her eyes flickered to Nia's badge and she winced. "I'm sorry, Dr. French. That was unprofessional of me."

"Don't worry about it," Nia answered automatically, though her attention was on the crowded doorway.

Inside the room Hart's voice barked a string of commands and the chaos gained a sense of order. From the hallway she could just see one of the patient's hands peeking out from beneath the sheet.

Marissa grimaced. "We're all tense these days, especially when we're monitoring one of the high-risk transplants. Like Julia here." Her voice softened on the name, saddened.

High-risk. It connected in Nia's head with an almost audible click. She turned to the nurse, who stared at the still figure on the bed with shadows crowding her broad face. "I'm sorry." Nia touched the other woman's arm when the tension inside Julia's room swung from hectic to frantic. "I'm sure you did your best. Rare-tissue-type patients don't have the best of prognoses to start with."

It was a fishing expedition cloaked in sympathy, and it made Nia feel faintly slimy. But this, like danger, was part of the job.

The nurse shook her head. "Julia was one of the lucky ones—or she should have been. She was rare type, but they found a match quickly. A really good match." In the room frantic turned to desperate, and Hart barked one order atop the next, sending nurses and junior doctors scrambling. But the bloodless fingers didn't move.

A vise tightened around Nia's lungs and heart. "She's rejecting?"

"She's dying," the nurse said flatly, turning away. "If you'll excuse me, I have other patients to tend." She hurried away and didn't bother to glance back as she slipped into a nearby ladies' room.

Nia understood. She always preferred to mourn in private, as well. But it wasn't the time to grieve for a stranger named Julia, or for the memories of another such room. It was time to do her job. Squaring her shoulders, she eased into the patient's room, grabbed a surgical mask and held it to her mouth as she slid along the back wall. As a visiting doctor she had the right. As an investigator she had the duty.

And as the woman bent on solving this case in spite of Rathe McKay and his outdated chauvinism, she had the need.

"Come on, Julia, don't quit on me now!" Hart's expression remained determined, but there was hopelessness in the faces around him as the Boston General staff worked to save the young, carrot-haired woman. Her skin was gray blue, the monitors around her nearly flat. Over the taint of antiseptic, Nia could smell death long before Hart called it.

"Time of death, thirteen-forty. *Damn* it." He stripped off his gloves and tossed them in the direction of a hazardous-waste bin. He stalked past Nia without acknowledging her.

She tried to move, but her feet wouldn't budge.

She should follow him. Talk to him. Confirm what Marissa and her ticking left eyelid had suggested, that this transplant patient was one who—on paper, at least—shouldn't have died. But Nia remained rooted to the spot, staring at the orange-haired girl on the bed and the nurses working on the still figure, moving slowly now that there was no rush.

But it wasn't a stranger's face Nia saw in the bed. It was her father's.

Her own.

Pain sliced into her lower back, sharper than it had been in the five years since the operation. She bit back a cry, pressed a hand to the scar on her belly, bolted from the room—

And crashed into Rathe.

RATHE GRABBED HER by the upper arms and felt terror morph to anger in an instant. He shook her. "Where the hell have you been?"

She didn't fight back, just sagged against him, which he found more unsettling than Cadaver Man's whispered threat. When an attendant shuffled out of a nearby patient's room and gave them a strange glance, Rathe muttered a curse, kicked a nearby supply closet open and dragged her inside. He flicked on the lights, shut the door and took a long, hard look at her, still not sure what had taken place in her office, what had happened just now.

She was pale. Her eyes were dark, stark holes in her head, and one hand was clamped to her side.

"You're hurt." It came out as more accusation than sympathy, and when he advanced with hands outstretched to check the wound, Nia backed away, sudden color flooding her cheeks.

"I'm fine." When he reached for her, she batted his hands away and snapped, "I said I'm fine. See? No blood." She lifted her dark, businesslike blazer to show him that the shirt beneath, wrinkled and smeared from when she'd been attacked in the lobby, bore no red stains.

She was unhurt. All the images that had raced through his mind when he saw the ransacked office bled away, leaving frustrated anger in their wake. She was okay. And he'd panicked needlessly. Unprofessionally. The knowledge sent him forward a step. "What do you think you're doing?"

The question brought her chin up, though the vulnerability lingered in her eyes. "What am I doing still working our case, do you mean? I'm working it because I'm staying, as you very well know." She lowered her voice and her color flared higher. "Don't blame me for calling Wainwright. You forced my hand."

"I'm not talking about bloody Jack Wainwright!" Rathe barked, advancing and feeling a spurt of triumph, or maybe shame, when she backed away. "I'm talking about here. Now." He cursed and scrubbed a hand over his short, spiky hair. Lowered his voice. "You weren't in your office."

And thank God for that.

"No, I wasn't." She sighed as though defeated. "I'm not going to hide there and wait for the case to solve itself, Rathe. I'm here to investigate, and I'm going to do my job with or without your help. Got it?"

He wasn't sure whether to kiss her or lock her in a

supply closet for the duration. The bloody woman made no sense, had no idea of the size of the tiger she was tweaking—either in him, or at Boston General.

"I got it," he snapped, "but I've got something else, too." He took her arm, opened the closet door, and ushered her none too gently out into the hall. "Come on. Into your office."

She balked. "We shouldn't be seen together."

"Doesn't matter," he replied, half dragging her down the hall. "Our cover's blown."

"What do you—" She stopped spluttering the moment he opened her office, urged her inside and locked the door behind them. She froze. Her color drained again. "What happened in here?"

"That's what I'd like to know." Now that he knew she was safe, Rathe felt the adrenaline leak out of him, leaving his chest empty and aching.

He brushed the tattered remains of a cheerful travel poster off the desk and sat, briefly wishing he was on that tropical island. Alone. Or perhaps with a woman who looked like Nia but didn't have her guts. Her lack of respect for seniority.

Her hell-bent determination to succeed in a dangerous profession.

"When did you find this?" She turned in a full circle, and he saw her eyes light on her gutted handbag and the empty envelope that had contained Talbot's lists of missing drugs.

"Five minutes ago, maybe less. I ran into your Cadaver Man downstairs and he called me by name. I came up here and found your office trashed." Remembered panic flickered at the edges of his mind, memories of the images his consciousness had drawn—Nia bound and gagged. Beaten for information she didn't have. Shot dead and left in a jeep outside HFH local headquarters as a warning. A taunt.

"I'm not her."

"What?" Rathe jolted his focus back to the ransacked office and found Nia watching him, her dark eyes steady and filled with a compassion he wanted no part of.

"I'm not Maria. This isn't Tehru. I can take care of myself."

Anger lashed through him, anger that she'd seen into him, anger that she knew what had happened to Maria and still couldn't tell that it was exactly the same. The danger was the same. "Is that what you call this?" He swept a hand toward shattered bookshelves. "Taking care of yourself? Just what were you doing while your office was being tossed? And why the hell didn't you lock the door?"

Her eyes narrowed. "I *did* lock the door. And for your information, I was watching a woman die. A rare-type kidney transplant rejected her organs and died, even though she was a high-risk case. She was young. Healthy. They found a donor quickly…"

Yet still she had died. Rathe felt a stab of sorrow for the patient, a slice of remorse for having manhandled Nia right after she'd run from the patient's room looking as if she'd seen—

What? A ghost? Something else?

He sighed. "Listen, Nia—"

"No, *you* listen, Rathe. I'm staying on this assignment no matter what you say. Our cover's blown? Then we'd better figure out how it happened. My office is trashed and my files stolen? Then let's start asking why someone doesn't want me to have Talbot's information, and how they got a key. A woman is dead?" She faltered and took a deep breath before continuing, "Then we're damn well going to figure out how and why, so we can stop it from happening again. Got it?"

He frowned down at her. "Pretty speeches won't get the job done, Nadia."

"No, but *I will.* And don't call me Nadia."

She walked to the corner of the office and stared down at her pillaged handbag. When she bent to retrieve it, he stopped her with a quick, "Leave it. We'll want Talbot and the detectives to see the mess."

She straightened. "Does that mean you're still on the case? You're not going to ask Wainwright to reassign you?"

"I'm on the case." Rathe scowled. "*We're* on the case. On one condition." He reached for the doorknob, needing to be somewhere, anywhere that wasn't two feet away from Nadia French.

Her eyes lit with a hint of the excitement he hadn't felt in a long, long time. The thrill of the hunt. "What condition?"

He stared at the blank wood of the door. "Don't mention Maria to me again. Ever."

FIVE MINUTES LATER, after she'd mastered both her irritation with Rathe and her grief for a stranger named Julia, Nia went in search of Logan Hart. She found the doctor in his office and tapped on the door frame. "Dr. Hart?"

He looked up from his paperwork, and his frown tilted up at the corners. "Dr. French, come in, please. And call me Logan."

"Then I'm Nia." As she sat she was surprised to realize that Logan Hart was actually quite attractive in a clean-cut, unlined fashion. Though he appeared only a few years younger than Rathe's chronological age, a decade or more could have separated them.

Of the two, Nia found Rathe far more attractive in a completely wrong-for-her sort of way.

He'd pushed her away seven years earlier, when she would have followed him anywhere. He'd abandoned her, and worse, he'd abandoned her father.

Given that, why did she still want to grab on tight and kiss him until he admitted there was something between them?

"Nia? Is everything okay?"

Flustered and suddenly warm, she waved a hand at Logan. "I'm fine. I'm just…" Just what? And why did it seem as though she'd spent the past three days assuring everyone she was fine?

"Still recovering from that nasty scene down in the atrium?" He leaned back in his chair, concern evident in his eyes. For some reason the expression didn't grate on her as it would coming from Rathe.

She inclined her head. "That, and someone trashed

my office while I was watching you work on your patient Julia."

Hart jolted. "You what? Who?" He lurched halfway to his feet then sat back down. He took a deep breath and pressed his palms to the desk. "Was anything taken?"

"Some of my working files." Nia shrugged, hoping he wouldn't ask why she'd kept her notes in the office. Rathe hadn't crucified her for the lapse, but she knew it had been a mistake. If the intruder had any doubt about her involvement in the case, those files had provided proof. "They're replaceable. My pocketbook was upended but nothing was taken."

"Which means it wasn't robbery." When she cocked an eyebrow, he shrugged. "It happens. This is a big hospital." He glanced at her, and Nia knew he was seeing the smudges on the collar of her once-white shirt. The wrinkles she'd tried to brush out and failed. "You've had a hell of a day, haven't you?"

His expression invited her confidence, but something held her back. Maybe it was the smoothness of his cheeks, marked with neither stubble nor character. Maybe it was the feeling that something was slightly…off in Hart's office. Or maybe it was the sudden realization that she'd made a grave tactical error. He'd been shocked by her earlier announcement, but he'd hidden it quickly. Naturally she'd assumed he was reacting to news of the break-in.

But what if he was more worried to hear that she'd seen the transplant patient die?

"It's been—it's been quite a day," she stammered as

the idea took root. Who better to warn Cadaver Man of the HFH investigation than someone inside Transplant? But why? And how did the patients figure in? The missing pharmaceuticals? She needed to know more about Logan Hart. More about the department.

"I'll phone those two detectives and have them look at your office," he promised. "Why don't you head back to the apartment building and get some rest? It's almost quitting time."

He knew where she was staying. And, as a ranking doctor, he could probably talk his way right past the guards in the lobby. Nia suppressed a quick shudder, then realized she could use it. She tilted her head down and glanced up at him. "I'll do that, thanks. But it's a little lonely there. And after what happened today..."

His eyes changed. Maybe they softened or maybe they took on a predatory gleam.

And maybe she was falling in love with her own theory and needed to back off until she had more facts.

"What about your...partner?"

"Rathe?" She shrugged. "He's an incredible investigator. But he's not exactly the kind of guy I'd choose to spend an evening with. He's not very warm and fuzzy."

Hart coughed, and she couldn't tell if he was covering a laugh. "Go home and get some sleep, you look bushed." He glanced at her, eyes betraying nothing. "There's a formal dinner tomorrow in honor of Director Talbot and his contributions to transplant medicine. I'll pick you up at seven." He lifted up the phone. "Right now I'll call the detectives, then find you another office to use."

"Thanks, Logan." She stood, mission accomplished almost too easily. "I think I'll follow the doctor's orders and quit for the night. It's been a long day."

She feigned a tired slump as she left, but once out the door, she turned right, away from the garage access. Maybe Logan was involved, maybe he wasn't.

But it didn't hurt for him to think she'd gone home when she planned on more snooping. If she could find a connection between him and Cadaver Man…

She'd have the case solved before Rathe knew what hit him.

LATER THAT NIGHT nerves and excitement thrummed in Nia's chest as the service elevator carried her down into the depths of Boston General. The doors slid open with a hiss, and she stepped out into the damp corridor. It was warmer than before, and machine noise echoed from every surface until she could hear almost nothing else. She took another step, heard her heels echo on the cement floor.

And heard something else behind her.

She spun, but not quickly enough. Strong fingers gripped her upper arms. A powerfully muscled leg wrapped around both of hers, and a firm, warm body pinned her against the wall, effectively neutralizing all her hard-learned defenses.

"You promised not to come back down here alone." Instead of shouting the words, Rathe nearly whispered them, his mouth near her ear, his breath warm on the side of her neck. His pulse, fast and strong, beat against her skin, reminding her of another time.

You promised to love me, was her first response, quickly stifled. Those had been empty words spoken in the heat of the moment, soon forgotten. And they had no place in the present. So she glared into the gray-blue eyes above hers, raised an eyebrow and said, "I lied."

His eyes darkened. They breathed in tandem, pressed together at hip and chest like lovers. He released her abruptly and stepped away. "Darn it, Nia—"

She held up a hand. "Don't start." She breathed past the ball of warmth in her stomach. "Now. Do you want to compare notes, or would you rather we run parallel investigations and waste time repeating each other?"

"Fine. Have it your way." He glared at her and finally backed down an inch. "But if anything happens to you, it's on your head, not mine."

"That's what I've been telling you all along." She crossed her arms and lifted her chin. "Now. What have you got?"

He stepped closer before he answered. She knew it was important that they keep a low profile, and they needed to shield their information from anyone listening in the deserted space, but the touch of his breath on the side of her face sent a rush of heat through her body. She held her ground, though she was equally torn between leaning in and running away.

"I had a look at the ID photo database in human resources," he murmured quietly. Nia didn't bother asking how. He'd either hacked his way in or charmed his way in. Either way, it was part of the job.

She tilted her head so her lips were just beside his ear, and whispered, "Did you find Cadaver Man's picture?"

Though they weren't touching, she could feel him tense. The thin layer of air between them vibrated with energy.

He leaned closer, until his cheek nearly grazed hers. "No. He wasn't on the maintenance roster. He's either working with a fake ID, or his records were deleted by someone higher up in the Boston General food chain."

So she and Rathe were thinking along similar lines. Nia smiled and whispered. "Speaking of which, I had a chat with Logan."

The air between them chilled. Rathe drew back an inch, his face blank. "Logan?"

"Assistant Director Hart." She frowned, stung by Rathe's sudden withdrawal, and by the unstated implication that she was being unprofessional by using the man's first name. "You know—young thirty-something, handsome." High up in the Boston General food chain.

"I know who he is, and I'll thank you to remember that I'm the senior investigator. When I want the administration to know something, I'll put it in my report." Rathe turned away, shoulders stiff. "Come on. As long as you're here, you can help me search. I have a feeling Cadaver Man was down here today for a reason, and I'd sure as hell like to know what it was."

Perplexed and oddly disappointed that he hadn't wanted to hear her theory, Nia stood in the damp, dim hallway and watched him walk away. What had just happened? For a moment there, he had seemed almost…

Jealous?

Ridiculous. She scoffed at herself. Hadn't she gotten over romanticizing the man a long time ago?

Apparently not.

Then he turned the corner to an intersecting corridor, leaving her alone in the noisy quiet. Nerves prickled to life on the back of her neck, and she rubbed her left eye when the skin around it tingled.

Resisting the urge to call him back, she strode toward the second hallway. She didn't run, but she didn't dawdle, either. Rathe seemed certain that Cadaver Man wasn't down there in one of the mazelike hallways.

But Nia wasn't so sure.

THEY SEARCHED the laundry subbasement for several hours and found exactly nothing. There was no sign of Cadaver Man or Short Whiny Guy, and no convenient stash of pilfered supplies awaiting transport out of the hospital to destinations unknown.

Even Nia's left eyelid had been quiet, which was both good and bad news. Good because that fleeting feeling of being watched had faded the moment she rejoined Rathe. Bad because it meant they were on the wrong track.

In uneasy accord they turned down yet another dimly lit corridor flanked with yet another phalanx of nondescript metal doors.

"You take that side." He gestured her to the left.

Nia nodded without a word. They hadn't spoken much. It seemed they'd said everything that needed to be said to each other. And if the thought was accompanied by a thump of disappointment, it was only because of her foolish fantasies from years ago, when she'd imagined she and Rathe would one day work side by side as partners. Lovers.

The reality was nothing like those dreams had been. The fantasy had been a silly amalgam of fleeting touches and hot, whispered promises. Of partnership and communication. The reality was damp, echoing hallways and strained silence.

And why was she thinking of this at all? He'd pushed her away. Worse, he'd pushed her father away when it counted most.

That was something Nia shouldn't forgive.

Repeating that thought in her mind, though it didn't echo as loudly as it had two days earlier, she pushed open the first door to begin the search. Rathe moved off down the hall while she checked her small room for anything suspicious—like a pile of the missing items from Talbot's list. But no such luck. The small space was a storage area of sorts, with row upon row of empty metal shelves. She sighed, locked the door and moved on to the next, preternaturally aware of Rathe's exact position relative to hers.

With her previous partners, Nia had consciously kept tabs on them in case they needed her help or she needed theirs. But with Rathe…she knew where he was at every moment. It was as though special McKay receptors had prickled to life on her skin, alerting her to his every motion, his every expression. Though she had her back to him, she could swear he was pensive.

Her left eyelid twitched.

"Hey!" Nia jerked a hand to her eye.

"What?" He was at her side in an instant. "What have you got?"

"I...I'm not sure. What were you looking at?" She prowled slowly up the corridor to where he'd been standing. He trailed her too close, and she almost asked him to back off. To give her room.

"I was checking out the end of the hallway. Something bothers me about it, but I can't quite figure out what." He moved past her and touched the wall with gentle, questing fingers.

Suddenly a long-suppressed sensory image of those fingers moving over her body swamped Nia. She pressed a hand to her jittery stomach and inhaled sharply.

A tendril of scent invaded her nostrils, sweet and tangy. Horribly familiar.

Blood. Death.

"Rathe, do you smell it?" She was almost unaware of him as she followed the scent to the third-to-last door.

"Nia, don't. Let me." His low, urgent words were lost to the tic of her eyelid and a feeling of impending panic. She shook off his restraining hand, opened the door, flicked on the light—

And screamed.

Chapter Five

Nia staggered back, away from the corpse. The man's throat was slashed from ear to ear. His clothes were soaked with blood, though the room was clean. And his eyes…his eyes had been cut from his head.

"Oh, God! It's Short Whiny Guy." Without thinking, without caring about what he thought of her, Nia grabbed on to Rathe and buried her face in his shirt, barely noticing when his arms came up and held her hard.

He cursed and toed the door shut with his boot before he bundled her toward the center of the building, half dragging her to the service elevators. "Come on. Let's get you out of here."

Nia let herself be shepherded for a moment. Then she dug in her heels and pulled away, stomach roiling. "Like hell. We need to stay down here and secure the scene. We have to call the cops so they can look at…at…" She held the back of her hand against her mouth, hoping the pressure could keep the nausea in.

She'd seen dead men before—the bodies of sick patients, victims of natural disasters, even soldiers killed by enemy fire. But this was different. This was cold. The throat wound was a single clean slice. The cuts that had removed Short Whiny Guy's eyes had been neat and precise. Almost surgical. Twin trickles of blood had run from the stark dark holes in his head and dried on his cheeks.

Like tears.

"Nia." Rathe's voice was quiet. Gentle. "You don't have to be here. I'll take you upstairs. We can call the others from there."

She stepped away and breathed through her mouth so she wouldn't smell the death. But it lingered, coating the insides of her nostrils and throat like bile. "I'll go up and call. You stay here with the body. If we leave and the killer comes back…"

They could lose the evidence that proved this was more than a few missing drugs and a cluster of transplant rejections. Something was going on at Boston General. Something deadly.

But Rathe shook his head. "He knows who we are, Nia. I don't want you going anywhere alone. Not now."

She didn't bother to argue, merely lifted her chin. "Then we both stay."

He held her eyes for a moment, then nodded. "Fine. We both stay."

When he turned away and punched a string of numbers into his phone, Nia let out the breath she'd been holding. She glanced down the hall, toward the room where they'd found Short Whiny Guy. She closed her eyes against the memory of the gaping bloody smile beneath his chin and the holes where his eyes should have been. He'd been left there for them to find, she was sure of it. But why? As a message?

Or a warning.

A FEW HOURS LATER Rathe and Nia met with the administrators and the cops in Director Talbot's office.

"I think we should turn the entire investigation over to the police," Logan said. "No offense to HFH," he nodded at Rathe and didn't meet his eyes, "but this is already beyond what we had envisioned."

The clock said 6:00 a.m. Rathe was bone tired, and if he was feeling it, Nia must be close to dropping. But being Nia, she'd refused to show her fatigue. She'd led the detectives to the dead man and watched as the corpse was photographed, bagged and wheeled out onto the loading dock for the body wagon.

Now, hours later, she was repeating the whole story once again for Director Talbot, the two Chinatown detectives and Assistant Director Hart—who had slid his chair closer to hers when he thought nobody was looking.

"And what had you envisioned?" She glared at Talbot. "That we'd come in, poke around for a few days and find nothing? Maybe the bad guys would get nervous? The supplies would stop disappearing and your survival percentages would miraculously increase?"

Though Rathe's gut still twisted at the memory of Nia's face when she'd run to him and clung, his lips twitched when Talbot frowned.

Score one for HFH. That's exactly what the director had thought.

"Listen here, Dr. French," Talbot began, only to be neatly interrupted by the younger of the two detectives.

"You can rest assured, gentlemen," Detective Peters's eyes flickered to Nia, "and lady, that we will actively pursue the murder of Arnold Grimsby." That had been the name finally attached to Short Whiny Guy. He'd had his license on him, but no ID. His name hadn't popped up in the hospital databases, which meant he didn't work at Boston General.

Yet he'd carried a hospital master key.

Rathe shifted in his chair. This was turning into a bigger case than he'd expected. At this point he'd be glad to hand the whole mess over to the cops.

But Nia pounced. "You said you'd investigate the murder. What about the missing supplies? The transplant rejections? It's all connected."

The detective frowned. "We can't be sure the murder is connected. Disappearing supplies are small potatoes, and a slight bump in transplant deaths isn't going to ring the chimes of our superiors. Though we'll keep your problems in mind, we're going to have to focus on the murder." He glanced at his partner, Sturgeon, who had remained in the back of the room, quietly sucking on a peppermint and observing the proceedings like a character from an Agatha Christie novel.

Sturgeon nodded and shifted the candy to his cheek. "Between budget cuts and man hours, we can't promise much."

"But Grimsby's *eyes were cut out!*" Nia slashed a finger at the older detective. "Doesn't that worry you?"

"Murder always worries me, Dr. French." Sturgeon's tired eyes were kind. "And, yeah, it's important. Maybe he saw something he shouldn't have. Maybe the killer wanted a souvenir." He pushed away from the wall. "Leave that investigating to us. And watch each other's backs. The guy who jumped Dr. French yesterday isn't talking—and he has himself a *very* expensive lawyer."

A junkie with a hotshot attorney. A dead man with a hospital master key. Rathe didn't like the connections his gut was drawing.

"I'm confused," Logan said, glancing between Nia and Rathe. "I thought the guy yesterday wanted money."

Peters inclined his head. "Dr. French's attacker is in custody, but he's not talking. It was probably just a mugging."

But when Peters glanced over, Rathe could see that neither of them believed that. He relaxed slightly, sensing an ally in the young detective. The young *married* detective.

"What if the attack was staged to keep me from seeing something?" Nia glanced from Talbot to Hart and back. "I was supposed to observe a rare-tissue-type transplant. What if the attack was meant to keep me away from the operating theater?"

Talbot half rose from behind his enormous desk. His eyes hardened. "Dr. French, *I* performed that surgery, and I resent the implication." The director of transplant medicine shot a fulminating glance at Rathe and the detectives.

Nia waited a beat, then quietly replied, "I meant no disrespect. But I wouldn't be doing my job if I didn't ask the questions."

Talbot harrumphed and sat back. "Yes, well. I know how much this investigation must mean to you, Dr. French, after what your father went through." He glanced at his watch. "Now, if you'll all excuse me, I'm presenting early rounds."

And just that quickly the meeting was over. When the others filed out, Rathe paused in the office, his mind locked on Talbot's comment about Nia's father. Tony had died of a heart attack.

Hadn't he?

Rathe caught the transplant director as he tried to slip out the back door of his office. "What does Nia's father have to do with this investigation?"

Brief irritation flashed in the older man's eyes, a strange-seeming response from an administrator whose department was linked to a murder. But just as quickly Talbot's expression shifted to harried worry. "There isn't a direct connection." He glanced at his watch again, making it clear he was late. "And my knowledge of her history is bound by doctor-patient confidentiality." He opened the door but paused before escaping through it. "However, you might want to ask yourself why Dr. French is on this case. And why she won't give it up."

Then he was gone, leaving Rathe wondering that very thing. He had assumed it was her innate drive, or perhaps her desire to show him up. But what if it was more? What if it was personal?

Then she'd be even more likely to endanger herself in pursuit of the truth.

On a curse, he spun and headed down the hallway after her. Damn it, he wasn't going to stand by and watch another partner die on a personal crusade.

He found her deep in conversation with Logan Hart. The doctor's tawny elegance countered her petite darkness nicely. He was young, steady and had a job that would bring him home for dinner safely every night.

He was everything Tony had once wanted for his daughter.

Rathe clenched his jaw when Nia nodded, smiled and parted from Hart with a half wave. Her voice carried when she said, "See you tonight, then."

Edgy irritation spiked through Rathe when she joined him, and they walked down the hall shoulder to shoulder. "Great. That's just what I need." They stopped outside her new office, and he cursed, not caring that they were attracting attention. "Did it occur to you that the middle of your first official investigation is *not* the time to start a romance?"

She shot daggers at him and lowered her voice. "And did it occur to *you* that we don't know who blew our cover?" She paused, and the implications surged through Rathe like guilt. Apparently his face reflected the emotion, because Nia nodded. "Right. Since theoretically only Wainwright and Boston General's head administrator and the transplant directors know about us, there has to be a leak high up. What better way to investigate—or use—the leak than cozying up to the assistant director?"

Nia's plan was devious. It was Machiavellian. It was manipulative. It was…

Exactly what Rathe would have suggested if he'd been thinking straight. Because she'd beaten him to it, he scowled. "Fine. But I'll be right behind you on your date tonight." He held up a hand to forestall her protest. "HFH policy, remember? Nobody goes Lone Ranger."

And with their cover blown and a murderer on the loose, he'd be sticking to her like a Band-Aid.

Rather than argue, she nodded, and he saw a flash of something in her eyes. Fear, perhaps, or regret. "Fine. But don't let him see you."

She turned away, but he caught her arm before she could leave. "Nia." He damned himself for needing to know, for breaking his own rule and getting personal. "What did Talbot mean about your father? When you called me back then, you said he'd had a heart attack."

Her eyes dimmed with old hurt. "The heart attack was a complication from kidney failure and a transplant." She lifted her chin. "Which you would have known if you hadn't hung up on me."

He wanted to turn away, wanted to run away. But he couldn't. She deserved better. She deserved the truth. "I couldn't come back, Nia. I promised him I wouldn't."

"I know. He told me." She dropped her voice but didn't look away from him. "That's what I didn't get to tell you—he forgave you. He forgave both of us. He wanted you to come back so he could tell you that before he died."

This time Rathe did turn away. He stared out the

sheer glass window, down at the small cars six stories below. He'd known Tony had forgiven him in the end. Somehow he'd known.

Hell, Tony never could keep a grudge. But part of Rathe had needed the reason to stay away from her.

He sighed. "It wouldn't have been real, Nia. It wouldn't have been right. I gave him my word that I'd never see you again." Never touch her again, taste her again. Never send her another silly trinket from a faraway land. Never ask her to share his life, homeless, rootless, living out of a half-packed duffel and dodging bullets. Murderers.

In the end he'd done her a favor. No woman needed to live his life. No woman should end up like Maria had.

Her voice was quiet, the hurt unmistakable. "Well, you kept that promise. I hope it keeps you warm at night, knowing that even though you refused to see him, my father died with your name on his lips." She turned, her shoulders set, and walked away without looking back.

After a moment Rathe followed.

UNWANTED TEARS clouding her vision, Nia slipped into the ladies' room, knowing it was one of the few places she could escape her partner's watchful gaze. There was a small alcove with a changing station and a single plastic chair. She sank into the chair, leaned her head against the cool wall and closed her eyes.

She'd known all along that her father had chased Rathe off—but nobody chased Rathe unless he was ready to run. At the time she'd been furious with her father, but even back then, when the hurt was fresh and new, she'd understood his reasoning. Her dad's experiences in the Army had marked him, made him fearful, and he'd wanted better for his little girl.

She hadn't agreed, but she'd understood. In the end, before he died, he'd understood, too, and he'd given her his blessing to do what she wanted to do with her life. What she *needed* to do. Because of that, and because she'd loved him so, she'd wanted to give her father one last gift before he died.

She'd wanted to give him his best friend back.

So she'd called Rathe and waited an age while HFH transferred her from one country to the next. She'd steeled herself against the sound of his voice and the immediate hint of wariness when he realized who was on the line. But she hadn't been prepared for him to refuse her request. He hadn't even given her an opportunity to pass on her father's message. He'd simply hung up.

And to learn that he'd guessed he was forgiven and still hadn't come home to her father's bedside, hadn't come back to her...

It shouldn't hurt so much. It merely confirmed what she'd known all along.

He hadn't *wanted* to come back. He might tell himself he'd wanted to keep a promise, and perhaps there was honor in that, but in the end it had been nothing more than an excuse.

"Damn him." Nia ground her palms against her eyes, trying to stem the tears that leaked between her fingers.

A toilet flushed nearby, and her cheeks heated at the

realization that she wasn't alone. A stall door closed, water ran briefly, and the air hand drier puffed to noisy life. After a moment, a wide, pleasant-looking face peeked into the alcove. Nia recognized Marissa, the nurse Logan had barked at during the previous day's transplant emergency.

The older woman seemed startled to recognize her. "I'm sorry, Dr. French. I'll leave you to your…thoughts."

"No. Wait." Nia sat up, wiped her face off and determinedly shoved Rathe from her mind. "I want to ask you something."

Marissa cocked her head. "Yes?"

"Yesterday morning Dr. Talbot performed a rare-type transplant. I was supposed to observe it but never got there." When the nurse merely lifted an eyebrow, Nia took a breath. "How is the patient?"

"He's fine, Dr. French. Still critical, of course, but hasn't shown any signs of rejection yet. Not like…" They both knew who she was thinking of. Logan's dead patient, Julia.

"Okay, thanks." Nia rested her head against the cool wall. Talbot's affront at her question had been the surgeon's ego talking, not guilt.

"Does this relate to your investigation?" The nurse's brown eyes shone with interest. "Do you have any suspects?"

Nia cocked her head, keeping it casual though her heart picked up a beat. "What investigation?"

"Oh, pish." Marissa waved a blunt-fingered hand. "Everyone knows that you and that handsome Dr. McKay are looking for the missing drugs. It's all over the hospital." She leaned against the wall as though settling in for a chat. "So, is Dr. Talbot one of your suspects?"

It was all over the hospital? Nia's fingertips tingled, as though she'd just touched a live wire. This was important. She was sure of it. "Who started the rumor about the investigation?"

Whoever it was had blown their cover and was, quite likely, the administrative leak she'd been looking for. She could bring the name to Rathe and they'd have their first solid lead. Well, their first lead aside from Short Whiny Guy's corpse, which was in the hands of the Chinatown detectives. They could lean on the leak, find Cadaver Man, and—

"It's no rumor." The nurse looked at her strangely. "Dr. McKay told us himself."

RATHE WAS BEGINNING to suspect Nia had crawled out the sixth-floor bathroom window to avoid him. But that was disproved when she blew through the door, ignored the elevators and jogged down the wide spiral staircase, lips set in a firm line.

"Now what is she doing?" he muttered as he followed her through the basement level morgue. He hoped she was observing the autopsy of Hart's dead transplant patient. He hoped she wasn't—

Damn it, she was. She stepped into the service elevator, the one that only went into the maintenance sublevels where she'd *promised* she wouldn't go alone, and the door eased shut.

Rathe was in the car and in her face before the doors

closed. "What the hell do you think you're doing? I told you not to come down here alone, damn it. I'm the primary on this case, and—"

She jerked her chin up and met him glare for glare. "Then why did you break our cover?"

He stopped. Swallowed. Noticed how near they were to each other and took a step back. "I beg your pardon?"

"I beg your pardon?" she mimicked him with a scowl. "Do you try to sound like you're sixty years old, or is it a natural talent? You're thirty-eight, Rathe. Knock off the crap and stop trying to compromise this investigation."

The doors groaned open. He grabbed her arm before she could leave the car. "What are you talking about?"

Her eyes burned him with fury, unshed tears and something he couldn't even name—maybe desperation?

"Our cover. You blew our cover. Why? So you could scare me into leaving? So you could prove your own warped theory about women? Well, guess what? I'm still here, a man is dead, and we've lost the element of surprise, thanks to you." She yanked her arm away and stalked out into the thrumming halls of the laundry level, which teemed with activity except where the police tape barred entry.

Shock rattled through him, followed by irritation. "Nia! Damn it, Nia, get back here."

She ducked under the police tape.

Cursing, Rathe followed. He snagged her arm, unlocked a nearby room, and pushed her into it, slamming the door behind them both. He didn't bother with the lights—the low glow of the emergency bulbs was sufficient for a fight. "Damn it, I didn't break our cover. Calm down and let's discuss this like professionals."

Except, so far she'd been the professional and he'd been wasting his energy trying to boot her off the case. He'd accused her of being hobbled by her sex, but he'd been the one keeping her from doing her job.

Her glare told him that and more. "Professionals don't betray their own partners."

"No," he said quietly, the fight draining out of him in an instant as the words echoed back to him in Maria's darker, huskier voice. "They don't." He set his jaw and stared at the featureless gray wall, seeing a lush rainforest canopy torn by machine gun fire. "Partners stick together, or they die. I learned that in Tehru. Which is why I'd never have blown our cover. I swear it."

He heard the screams in his mind, smelled the taint of blood and explosives.

Nia sighed and uncrossed her arms. "This is not about Maria. This is about us and our investigation." She stuck her hands in her pockets. "But damn it—if you didn't break our cover, then who did? And why did the nurse think it was you?"

He shrugged. "Someone posed as me, maybe, or someone lied. Maybe even the nurse." Though he didn't think it likely.

"I'm sorry. I shouldn't have jumped to conclusions." She turned away. "I just...I'm confused. And I'm frustrated."

Her scowl and the defeated droop of her shoulders should have thrilled him. It was what he wanted—for her to learn that Investigations wasn't all about excitement and adventure. Mostly, it was hard work and aggravation. He'd wanted her to lose interest in the work. He should be feeling victorious.

Instead he was vaguely disappointed in her. He chose his words carefully. "It's not supposed to be easy. If it were, I'd be out of a job."

She shot him a filthy look. "I'm not talking about the case, McKay, I'm talking about your attitude. About how everything I do or say eventually comes back to Maria and the guilt you feel over her death." She held up a hand to forestall his protest. "I'm not trying to excuse myself for what just happened. I should have known better than to believe you'd knowingly endanger us—even if it meant getting me off the case. But we're going to have to come to some sort of agreement here, or this is going to be impossible."

Helpless guilt battled regret in his chest, then bumped into denial. He forced them all down and found himself asking, "What sort of agreement?"

Instead of answering directly, she sighed and said, "Tell me about her."

The quiet request rattled him. It had been a long, long time since he'd consciously remembered that time, though flashes of it had been intruding steadily for days, ever since Nia had reentered his life.

It was a long moment before he said, "How much of it do you already know?"

"Only what I overheard." She leaned against the gray wall beside him, so they were both facing the door, not touching, but near enough so her heat warmed his arm. "My father told me the exciting stories at first. Then, once I started talking about premed and self-defense classes…"

Rathe knew. The stories had stopped because Tony hadn't wanted his daughter anywhere near HFH. Anywhere near *him* and the danger that went with the lifestyle.

And, damn it, he'd been right.

She touched his hand. "Tell me."

She deserved to know, Rathe decided, because it was a main part of why he'd left her years ago. And maybe if she understood, she'd be more careful. Maybe she'd stay alive.

He took a breath. "Maria and I met during HFH training, both fresh out of med school." He tried to picture her face but failed. "We became partners first, then lovers." Which had been his first, and worst, mistake. He hadn't been able to separate partner from lover. "She was beautiful and independent, like you." But Maria had been aloof and reserved, whereas Nia wore her emotions like a badge.

Which made her even more vulnerable.

"What happened?" Her gentle prompt brought him back.

"We'd been a month in the Tehruvian back country during a period of nasty civil unrest. Maria and I traveled from village to village with a group of HFH doctors, treating patients wherever we could. There were so many wounded—" He broke off and stared into the shadows. "And there were too many factions, all struggling for control of that little slice of jungle. Maria…had political leanings. She sympathized with one of the rebel groups." HFH was supposed to remain neutral, but Maria hadn't cared. She had her convictions and nobody, certainly not Rathe, could tell her otherwise. "She befriended one of the leaders." Perhaps had been his lover. "We fought about it nearly every day, and when he called her to treat patients inside the military camp…she went."

The last time he'd seen her alive, clinging to the back of a jeep, she'd flipped him off as if to say, *I'm through with you and your rules. Take that!*

He was aware of Nia at his side, aware that this was only the second time he'd told this story. The first was to her father. She took his hand, and warmth traveled up his arm. She smelled like stability. Home. All those things he couldn't care about, living the life he'd chosen.

"Go on."

He breathed through his nose and pushed himself past the rest of it. The worst of it. "The rebel faction she was traveling with was ambushed by another group. Maria and her friends were executed. She was delivered to HFH as a warning that we should stay out of their country, their business." She had been bound and gagged. A small bullet hole had marred her smooth cool forehead, an explosive exit wound had gaped at the back. He swallowed. "We pulled out the next day."

He'd run, leaving her killers unpunished. Though the rebel factions had later been conquered and their various leaders imprisoned, the knowledge had been little comfort. Rathe would always know he'd run.

Nia pulled her hand away and swung around to face him. In her eyes Rathe saw both sympathy and an unexpected bite of temper. "I'm sorry, Rathe. That must have been awful, and there's nothing I can say to take away the memories. But you seem to be forgetting that it was her choice to go. Just as it's my choice to stay. You're not responsible for either of our decisions."

The snap in her voice startled Rathe, irritated him. When Maria's body was dumped off, he'd nearly gone mad, knowing he'd been to blame. He stepped toward Nia and scowled. "What do you know about it? You were just a kid when it happened. Hell, you're still a kid now!"

Her eyes narrowed on a hint of wetness, though he wasn't sure whether it was anger or tears. "I'm the same age you were when Maria chose to go off with the rebels."

He set his teeth. "I should have stopped her." *She should have listened to me.*

Though he didn't say the words aloud, Nia seemed to read them in his face. Her eyes softened. "Loving someone doesn't mean doing everything they say, Rathe."

Love. It was a word he hadn't consciously thought in years. Not since his best friend had punched him in the face and loaded him onto a plane with orders never to see Nia again.

Well, he was seeing her. She was right in front of his face, twice as beautiful as she'd been seven years earlier. Twice as stubborn.

"Maria died because I mixed up my personal feelings with my professional responsibilities. No," he touched a finger to her lips and felt the slow burn of blood through his veins, "let me finish. As an HFH doctor, I should have reported her and had her yanked the moment she took up with him. As a man—" a *young* man, as Nia had pointed out "—I thought I could win her back."

"Yet you didn't fight for me when my father sent you away." She swallowed hard. "You just…went."

He didn't bother to deny it. Nor did he bother to deny the rising heat between them, the tension that came from what had happened between them before, what was coming between them now. He nudged up her chin with his fingertip. "I'm here now. But I won't mix personal and professional aspects ever again. So you choose. Partners or lovers?"

Before she could frame an answer, he bent and kissed her, swallowing her startled gasp and nudging his tongue between her lips.

Remember what we had before, he meant the kiss to say. *Think of what we could have now.* Then her flavor exploded on his tongue, rich and potent, and his mind went blank, save for one guilty thought.

He had promised. But sometimes, a man had to break a promise to keep a promise. He'd promised to stay away from her, but he'd also promised to keep her safe. What if he could only save her by becoming involved?

So he poured himself into the kiss. The sensations reminded him of the blessed time they'd shared in an airport hotel. His hands traced her body, telling her of the sleepless, lonely nights that separated them, the sleepless nights they could pass together.

A noise from outside the room was a vague intrusion, quickly lost in the feel of her neat, narrow hands gripping his shirt…and pushing him away.

"Damn it, Rathe." She lifted a trembling hand to her flushed, swollen lips. Her chest heaved as though she'd run a mile, and her eyes narrowed suspiciously. "That's not fair."

Heartbeat pounding in his temples, he closed the distance between them, knowing he'd won, knowing she felt the same way she had seven years earlier. Knowing he could use it.

He brushed a strand of hair away from her cheek. "I'm not trying to play fair. I'm trying to make up for lost time. So tell me…" He imagined her beneath him, surrounding him. Safe. "Partners or lovers?"

She lifted her chin. Her lips drew a flat line across her face. "Partners."

And she turned and walked away. The action startled him, disappointed him and brought back an echo of the pain he'd felt when the hotel door closed on her heels the day he'd sent her away for her own good.

In his mind Rathe heard the rev of a badly tuned jeep and a scattering of gunshots. But in the small room he heard Nia curse.

In that instant personal tension shifted to trepidation. "What is it?"

She swallowed, hand on the doorknob. "The door won't open. We're trapped."

Chapter Six

Stupid, stupid, stupid. Nia stuffed down the fear and yanked on the storage room door. She'd been stupid to stop paying attention to the danger, and stupid to think, even for a moment, that Rathe's kiss had been genuine.

He'd found another angle to work, that was all. Another way to ease her off the case. *Partner or lover.*

Worse, she'd been so caught up in the moment, in the memories, that she'd done the unthinkable—let down her guard and allowed Cadaver Man or one of his accomplices to trap them in a tiny room.

Stupid. She let the self-recrimination beat back the flutter of panic. Sweat prickled at her nape. She wasn't sure which was worse, the thought of being trapped in here with Rathe or the thought of what might await them on the other side of the door.

"Here, let me." When he nudged her aside, his touch scalded her flesh, but she shook it off and pressed her ear to the door. She swore she could hear a laundry cart rumbling past, down a corridor that was supposedly off-limits.

Rathe cursed and kicked the door, more from frustration than a plan, and turned away. "I don't suppose HFH training includes lock picking these days?"

"It's not the lock." Nia twisted the knob freely and resisted the urge to beat against the thick metal and scream. She took a deep breath, willed her heart to slow. "I think someone wedged the door on the other side."

"Great." Rathe scowled. "Then what's your plan, *partner?*"

Nia felt a prickle of surprise at the temper in his voice, the anger etched into the lines of his face. He was annoyed she'd rather be his partner than his lover. Of all the nerve!

Irritated, she glared at the door and saw that it was hung from the inside. Bingo. "I think I can get us out of here." She pulled the small tool kit from her back pocket, unable to resist adding, "And for the record, there's a big difference between Maria and me. I put the job first."

Rathe muttered something uncomplimentary. For a man who railed about women being unprofessional, he seemed to be having a hard time with the concept himself. Professionals didn't go around kissing each other.

Offering themselves as lovers.

Ignoring the flare of warmth that buzzed through her body, ignoring the taste of him on her lips and the imprint of his flesh on hers, Nia positioned a small screwdriver, tapped it with her collapsible hammer and neatly popped the door hinges. "Here," she ordered, "you grab the door and I'll keep watch."

It wasn't the first time her tool kit had come in handy and it likely wouldn't be the last. She folded the worn leather neatly and passed a hand over her father's initials. *Thank you, Daddy.*

He might not have understood why she wanted to join HFH, but in the end he'd tried to support her as best he could. Because she'd loved him, and because she believed Rathe had loved him, too, she could understand part of Rathe's decision not to come home.

But not all of it.

"I don't hear anything." With one hand on the doorknob and the other on the upper hinge, Rathe eased the heavy metal slab aside. "Be careful."

But the hallway was empty save for a strand of yellow police tape. No Cadaver Man armed with a scalpel and a penchant for eyes. No laundry cart filled with pilfered supplies. Nothing.

Adrenaline drained away, leaving Nia hollow.

"Well, hell." Rathe toed the wooden chock that had held the door shut. "Someone wanted us out of the way."

"Or they wanted us trapped until they were ready to deal with us." Her voice quavered with the memory of bloody tear tracks, but she forced herself to stand away when Rathe moved up beside her. She squared her shoulders. "Let's do our job. You've got my back, partner."

"Nia…" His tone was low with warning, but she ignored it and him and set off down the hall, toward the room where they'd found the body.

Nerves sizzled to life on every exposed inch of her skin. Her eye twitched like quick butterfly wings when she neared the room. If Rathe hadn't been right behind her, she might have turned and run for the elevator, but she forced herself to forge onward.

Her hand trembled as she reached for the doorknob. The police seal was broken, the door half-ajar. Someone had been inside.

Perhaps they still were.

Excitement thrummed through her body, thundered in her ears. Fear was an echo of nerves, held at bay by the man at her heels. Her partner.

She pushed the door open.

The room was empty. Only a dark, dried smear, a smudge of chalk and a dusting of powder marked where the body had been. But the tension grew worse.

She eased back and let the door swing closed. "Earlier, when we were…" Arguing. Talking about Maria. Kissing like seven years hadn't passed. "…Occupied, I thought I heard something in the hall."

"I heard a thump." Rathe's eyes were dark with a potent combination of anger and the same things she was remembering.

"No. After that." Nia cast back over her scattered impressions, tried to blunt the memory of his kiss, of the way he had made her feel, as though she was all he'd ever wanted. All he would ever need.

She knew better than that. He would always pick the job over her, so she'd beaten him to it.

And it was on that thought that she heard the sound again. Rathe gripped her shoulder tightly and jerked his chin in the direction of the noise. "Do you hear it?"

She nodded and dropped her voice to the level of his, near a whisper. "A laundry cart." She glanced at him. "Do you believe me now?"

"Come on. This time you can watch my back—partner." And he was off, walking cat's-paw quiet on his rubber-soled boots.

Heart beating an excited tattoo, Nia followed on tiptoes, careful not to let her low heels tap the echoing floor. The noise grew louder, then faded again, as though the cart had turned a corner. But there was no corner to turn. The short hallway dead-ended.

"Damn it." Rathe thumped the wall in frustration, the noise echoing strangely in the closed-in space. "We're missing something."

She checked the doors on either side of the dead end. Empty storerooms. "Let's work our way around to the next corridor over. Maybe the sounds are traveling from there."

"Fine." He scrubbed both hands through his silvery-blond hair, leaving the short strands sticking up on end. It made him look younger. The sight tightened a fist around her heart at the thought of what might have been.

"Focus," she muttered to herself as she ducked beneath the police tape. "Do your damn job."

"What was that?"

She glanced over her shoulder at Rathe. "Nothing." But she could see in his eyes that he understood, perhaps too well. Something had changed between them the moment he'd told her about Maria. But if the confession had eased his soul, it had done the opposite for hers, because now she knew for sure.

He still loved Maria. Probably always would. It was in his eyes when he spoke of her—the anguish and the betrayal. The love.

It was how Nia had once imagined him looking at her.

Back in the main laundry area, the human noise was louder, the pace more frantic. She picked her way through a sea of canvas-sided carts, peering into each just in case. But instinct drew her onward, past the washing machines and giant steamers, past the rows and racks of pristine white lab coats and folded towels. Through a sea of workers, who carefully ignored the investigators, then whispered when they were past.

Rathe followed her, ghostlike, as she doubled back to the section of corridor she imagined was immediately opposite the dead end. It was guarded by a heavy metal door and a spray of caution signs.

She paused. "The incinerator?" Instantly her mind conjured images of fiery pits and screams. *Focus.* This wasn't a B-grade action movie, it was Boston General Hospital.

Still, her shoulders were tense with anticipation when she eased open the door. Her left eyelid pulsed.

The walls were thick, and nearby doors opened to daylight. The incinerator was built into the outer wall of the hospital, separate, yet not, lest the fire run amok. Nia shivered at the thought of a hospital in flames.

"See anything?" Rathe crowded in behind her, making her feel simultaneously safe and unsafe.

She stepped farther into the narrow room and heat bloomed across her body. Her eyes locked on a canvas cart. "There's a laundry cart. Think someone's been burning clothes?"

The small space was empty, but for the cart in the corner. Nia's eyes were drawn to a scrap of paper caught in the door of the idling incinerator. Rathe headed for the laundry cart while she bent to read the tiny letters.

Luer Lock Syr—

"Hey! I think I've got something." When Rathe turned in inquiry, Nia spun the wheel on the incinerator door. It opened on a wash of hot fumes. The beast might be quiet at the moment, but its insides pulsed with radiant heat, and the air steamed when warmth rushed outward. A red light blinked on the console, warning Nia that the machine hadn't yet cooled down to safe levels.

Yeah, like she couldn't tell that from the blast of hot air.

Disregarding the danger and the foul fumes, Nia used her fingernails to tease the scrap of paper free. More of the label was visible now. Luer Lock Syringes 1 CC.

"The supplies!" She turned toward Rathe to share the discovery. "We've found the—*look out!*"

An apparition lunged up from the laundry cart and tackled Rathe. Trailing a white sheet, it could have been Jacob Marley's ghost, but the solid smack of flesh on flesh was real. The laundry cart overbalanced with a crash. Taken by surprise, Rathe fell beneath the weight of his gray, ghostly attacker.

Nia screamed before she realized the heavy metal door would muffle the noise. There would be no help from the others in the laundry area.

Heart pounding, she leaped aside as the men rolled across the floor, grunting and trading punches like dirty street fighters. Cadaver Man kicked the tangling sheet aside, and Nia grabbed it.

"Get up, Rathe. *Get up!*"

Either he heard her cries, or realized he had no leverage on the floor. Rathe elbowed the taller man in the gut, scrambled to his feet and shot her a wild look. "Get out of here."

"Like hell I will." When Cadaver Man lurched to his feet and swung a meaty roundhouse at Rathe's head, Nia stepped in and looped the sheet across the villain's throat. She jumped on his back, pulled tight and did her best to strangle him.

Mistake. Cadaver Man roared, spun and slammed himself backward against the incinerator console. The blow drove the breath from Nia's lungs in a whoosh that was masked by the scream of sirens and the roar of machinery as the incinerator flared to life.

A gout of heat and smoke belched from the open door, then the failsafes shut down the metal dragon. Still, the heat in the room skyrocketed, the metal glowed cherry red.

"Nia, let go!" Before her dazed muscles could obey Rathe's shout, he hit Cadaver Man from the side, sending the three of them staggering toward the open door of the incinerator.

Instead of letting go, she tightened her fingers on the sheet and her knee grip on Cadaver Man's ribs. She jerked her weight to the side, hoping he would overbalance.

He did. Right into the incinerator.

The lean gray man shot his hands out and touched hot metal. Steam rose. Flesh sizzled. And Cadaver Man screamed, a high, thin noise of agony.

He spun and shuddered, bucking Nia off his back. She felt the sheet skim through her fingers, felt her body lift through the air.

Furnace-hot air blasted around her.

Gravity slammed her toward the ground, toward the red-hot metal. She reached out her hands; twisted her body and fought the inevitable.

"Nia!" The shout was almost lost in the machine's roar.

"Rathe!" She felt his fingers tangle in her shirt and yank. Buttons popped, cloth ripped. She grabbed for him, and their hands locked. They tumbled to the floor—

Outside the incinerator.

The cement was cool at Nia's back, Rathe warm against her front. They lay chest to chest, tangled together like lovers.

Cadaver Man was gone.

Rathe lay still, his heart pounding in time with hers. Quick and frightened. Excited. After a moment he groaned and buried his face in her hair. "I can't take this, Nia. You're scaring the hell out of me with these stunts. You're a bloody menace!"

But there was no censure in the words now. There was only weary acceptance. So she took a chance. "I'm also a bloody good investigator. Admit it."

They had evidence now, and connections. Cadaver Man formed a link between the corpse and the missing supplies. But who did he work for? How did the transplant deaths fit in?

And why burn the pilfered equipment? Or had they just burned the packages? And if so, *why?*

"Damn it, Nia—"

The rest of his words were lost in the metal howl of the outer door, and the arrival of the ERT—the equipment response team. Summoned by the incinerator's alarm, they were stunned to find a pair of doctors on the floor, surrounded by crumpled whites and an upended laundry cart.

As soon as she could, Nia slipped away from the chaos, out the back door, which opened onto the loading area. She tucked the scrap of paper in her pocket and wished that it had been something more concrete. More obvious. But she couldn't think about it now; she was suddenly too tired. Achingly bone-weary, fuzzy-head tired. Too tired to even face the drive to the apartment.

Call it delayed shock, call it lack of sleep or adrenaline letdown, her body was shutting down. She stumbled to the curb and belatedly realized she was alone—and Cadaver Man had escaped through the same door. He could be anywhere. He could be—

A hand gripped Nia's upper arm. She squeaked before recognizing the flare of warmth.

"It's me." Rathe cupped her elbow in one warm hand. "I'm taking you home." He flagged a passing cab.

"You don't need to."

"Maybe not, but I'm going to, anyway. Your daddy raised me right." He slid into the cab beside her and gave the driver the address of the Boston General apartment building.

Though it seemed she should take offense to his high-handedness and that last comment, Nia couldn't stir up a good dose of anger. Her body wanted to shake with the memory of plunging toward the incinerator's gaping maw. Her eyes wanted to tear with frustration that they were still so far away from a solution. And her heart wanted to ache with what she'd seen in Rathe's eyes when he'd held her pinned to the floor. After he'd saved her life.

"Rathe..." she began, not sure what she meant to say.

"Shh. We'll talk about it later. Trust me."

And strangely enough, she did.

RATHE GOT HER HOME, bullied her into bed and closed the bedroom door behind him. He didn't sneak in later and watch her sleep, though part of him wanted to do just that. He didn't kiss her good-night, either. It wouldn't have been professional.

And a man could only take so much.

Instead he ordered a pizza, commandeered the neutral-toned living room couch and the sturdy coffee table and got to work. He snagged blank paper from Nia's portable printer and used a pencil to chart their clues and conjectures. Connections and interconnections.

And if his mind wandered to the bedroom down the hall, imagined her naked and sprawled amidst the warm sheets, it was only proof of his tenet. Women didn't belong in HFH investigations. They were a distraction. A liability.

But the mantra rang false in his head. Nia wasn't the problem here, he was. When he'd asked her to pick, she had chosen the job over him. And it stung.

"Rathe?"

His eyes snapped up. The pencil between his fingers cracked in two. She stood in the hallway, messy-haired and clad now in a waterfall of silk that glowed primary colors against the oatmeal apartment decor. That image instantly, irrevocably banished the memory of a teenage college student sitting on the beach steps behind him. It banished the mental snapshot he'd kept of that last morning in the airport hotel, when he'd woken up before her, fever broken, fully aware of where he was. Who she was. What he'd done.

And how much he wanted to do it again.

But those images were now replaced with the sight of womanly curves, dark, tumbling hair and sleepy eyes. In that instant she went from being Tony's daughter to being a woman. Heaven help him.

She nodded to the papers strewn across the coffee table. "Find anything?"

"Nothing jumps out at me." He grabbed a slice of cold, congealed pizza, more to keep himself from reaching for her than from hunger. "I figure Arnold Grimsby—Short Whiny Guy—was killed to keep him from talking…but about what? Are the missing pharmaceuticals really connected to the transplant deaths? If so, how? And why burn them?" He shook his head in disgust and tossed the pizza down without taking a bite. "We need more."

"Then we'll get more." She glanced at the clock above the blank TV set. "Logan's picking me up in an hour. Maybe you should search his office while I keep tabs on him. Better yet, search his house."

"We'll stay together." There was no way he was leaving her alone with Hart.

"But—"

"This isn't negotiable, Nia." He rose to his feet and paced, needing to work off the excess energy that had buzzed through him from the moment she appeared in the hallway door and his mind had pictured her naked beneath the robe. "Cadaver Man has inside information and free access. That has to come from somewhere, right? And the jerk who attacked you hired himself a fancy lawyer. Big money. That says doctor to me."

She crossed her arms. "You're falling in love with your own theory, Rathe. And you're reaching."

"Of course I'm reaching." He rubbed both hands across his face. "What else can I do? We need more evidence."

"Exactly. Which is why you should snoop in Logan's office while I keep him occupied. I don't necessarily think he's our man, but there was something… strange about him when the transplant patient died. I think he knows something."

"I'm not leaving you alone with him." Rathe crossed the room, stopping just a heartbeat away from her. "I won't."

She lifted her chin, irritation chasing the sleep from her eyes. "You would if I were a man."

"Nia…" She was right and they both knew it. She pursed her lips, and the sight went straight to his groin. Drawn by the invisible bonds that bound them one to the other, he leaned down, damning the consequences. She swayed toward him, just a whisper away, slid both hands up his chest—

And pushed him away.

"Back off, Rathe. Partners or lovers, remember? It's your rule, so I suggest you stick to it." She spun and retreated in a flash of colored silk and bare legs. The bathroom door shut behind her. Moments later the shower splashed to life.

Leaving Rathe alone. Aching.

No, that wasn't right. He was simply alone, as he'd been for so much of his life except for two bright spots—the time he'd shared with Maria, and those years he'd fancied himself a member of Tony's family.

"Damn it." He scrubbed a hand across his face. Fatigue tugged at him. A brief catnap had done him little good. He was tired, not just from this assignment, but from the grind of the life. The endless stream of temporary friendships. The never-ceasing danger.

Maybe Wainwright had a point. Maybe the great Rathe McKay was finally burning out. Maybe it was time for him to take a desk and leave the field to new, enthusiastic investigators. Like Nia.

His jaw clenched and he glared at the closed bathroom door, forced himself not to imagine slick pink flesh and dark, wet hair. He forced his stiff legs to carry him back to the couch, forced himself to pick up his handwritten notes and read them for the tenth time. Forced himself to focus.

And he saw the connection.

Chapter Seven

Nia shaved her legs, slathered herself with scented lotion, and felt foolish for taking the time. This wasn't a date, it was business.

But she couldn't quell the low hum of excitement in her stomach as she slid on the one black dress she'd brought with her and tweaked her killer black garters into place. She piled her dark hair atop her head and fastened it there with two faux diamond combs, providing a hint of flash that was echoed at her throat and ears. She slipped into low black shoes with soft rubber soles—perfect for running, if necessary—and stepped back to approve her appearance in the wide wardrobe mirror.

She didn't clean up often. But she cleaned up well.

It wasn't until she turned for the door and the excitement balled in her throat that Nia jolted, finally realizing that she wasn't excited to see Logan, wasn't excited about taking this next step into covert work.

No, she was excited for Rathe to see her. Excited for him to realize what he'd been missing these past seven years.

"Knock it off and focus," she told herself, "you've outgrown him. This is about the job, not about Rathe."

But that didn't settle the anxious knot in her stomach, nor did it stop her from striking a pose just inside the living room.

He didn't even glance up from his papers. "I think I've figured it out."

Her excitement shifted directions. She crossed the room and leaned over him. "What? Tell me?"

"I think it's black market." He turned toward her. "I'll bet—" He froze, his eyes locked on the neckline of her dress, which hadn't seemed daring only moments before.

Heat suffused Nia's body. Her nipples crinkled to points beneath the lacy black demibra. She slapped a hand to her throat, where the material gapped, and stumbled back a pace. Her face burned from the heat, and from the sudden flare in his eyes.

"But—" She cleared her throat against a sudden tug of wanting. "But why would Cadaver Man incinerate the supplies if he could sell them?"

"I'm not talking about the supplies." Rathe shook his head. "I think a few boxes were burned to misdirect us." His eyes bore into hers, and it felt as though they were having two separate conversations. Their voices were discussing the case, but their bodies had moved on to an entirely different topic.

A more dangerous one.

"Then what?" She took another step back. He stood and followed with a single stride forward, making her feel like prey.

"The organs. Rare-type organs have a huge black market value, especially if you have a transplant doctor willing to do the work himself."

It made a horrible sort of sense, but didn't account for everything. "How would it work? The Boston General patients are receiving their transplants. We're not missing organs, we're losing patients." Like Julia. Somehow the woman's name, her face, had stayed with Nia.

"I know. The autopsy on the last dead patient showed a proper transplant—two failing kidneys and the new one grafted lower down. So we're not missing organs...." He dragged a hand through his hair. "But I pulled in a marker and got a copy of last month's transplant list. I compared it to the one Talbot gave us from the current database and found two patients who'd fallen off the list." He handed her a sheaf of papers. Two vaguely familiar names were highlighted. "These guys are big money." He paused. "Big, *dirty* money."

The implication was horrifying. Nia set the papers down and backed away. "But you said it yourself— we're not missing organs. Illegal transplants might account for the missing drugs, but how could someone sell organs out of Boston General without it being obvious?"

"Maybe they're not coming out of Boston General. Maybe they're coming from somewhere else."

The whole notion was something out of an urban legend, with patients waking up in strange hotel room bathtubs missing a kidney.

At the thought, Nia's lower back twinged a protest.

She held up her hands. "That's pure conjecture. Where's your proof?" She gestured to the names. "What if these two died? It happens." Too often.

"And what if they're alive?"

"I don't know." Nia pinched the bridge of her nose. She couldn't comprehend the selling of body parts, though she knew it happened from time to time. What sort of person could be involved in such a thing? What evil could cause a doctor to auction off an organ that rightfully belonged to the next tissue match on the list? "What if we—"

A knock sounded at the door, interrupting.

An unaccountable chill swept across her nearly bare shoulders, and she thought of Hart's eyes as he'd worked to save the patient's life. He'd been cool as he worked. Almost dispassionate. At the time she'd attributed it to the reserve a surgeon needed to stay a step away from his patient's pain. From the failures.

Now, she wondered.

A second knock sounded, then Hart said, "Nia? It's me. Logan. Are you ready for dinner?"

"You don't have to go," Rathe said quietly. He closed the distance between them and ran a gentle finger down her cheek, leaving a new set of shivers behind. "You can say you're sick, stressed, not in the mood. You've had a busy few days—he'll understand."

And Rathe would understand, too. She saw it in his eyes. He wouldn't think her weak or womanly, or if he did, he'd never say it. Something had changed in him, though she wasn't sure if it was because of the acknowledged chemistry that pulsed between them or if he was truly beginning to accept her as a partner.

But it didn't matter. This wasn't about his opinion. This was about her job. About saving lives.

She shook her head. "I'm fine. I'll go."

Another knock. "Hello? Are you in there?"

Eyes locked with Rathe's, Nia raised her voice. "Sorry, Logan. I'm running behind. I'll be there in a minute!"

"Nia, please. Stay home. I have a bad feeling about this." As though he had the right, Rathe cupped the curve of her hip with one wide, warm hand.

The rasp of cloth and sensation scraped along her nerve endings, and she fought not to jerk away. A pulse shot to her core, making her almost painfully aware of the naked skin above her garters and the narrow strip of silk between.

She stepped away. "Don't patronize me. We both know this is our best chance of getting information. I'll keep Logan busy while you search his office. Set your phone to vibrate—I'll call when we're ready to leave." His eyes reflected a potent combination of indecision and dark heat, and she softened her voice. "It's an awards ceremony. I'll stay with the crowds, I swear. I'll be fine."

It was an empty promise and they both knew it, but after a moment Rathe nodded. "I'll follow you there and wait until you're inside. Buzz me twenty minutes before you'll be ready to leave. I don't want you alone with him."

This time when he cupped her hips in both his hands, she didn't pull away. Heat flared through the soft black material and Nia's internal muscles pulled tight into a greedy, needy knot. A cough outside the heavy door reminded her they were not alone, and she lifted her hands to Rathe's chest.

"Rathe. I've got to go."

"I know." But neither of them moved. Rustling and a shift of feet in the hallway carried to them clearly, making it feel as though their almost embrace was public. "Be careful."

She tossed her head. "Of course."

"No. I mean it. Be careful." His eyes bore into hers. "If anything happened to you…"

Her stupid, feckless heart shuddered when he faltered. "Yes?"

"Aw, hell." On an oath, he closed the distance, trapping her hands between them when she would have held him away. "Be careful."

And he kissed her. Hard.

It was the third time he'd kissed her in so many days. It should have been familiar enough that she could break away and remind him that they were partners before she whirled and made a grand exit.

And she'd do that, Nia decided. In a minute.

Right then she was busy. Her fingers were busy tangling in his shirt, exposing a slice of warm, taut flesh. Her lips were busy parting beneath his, her tongue busy rubbing against his, exploring, tasting, learning. Logan coughed again in the hall and she wished him gone.

She heard Rathe groan and wished him naked. Heat speared through her, lust arrowed to the strip of silk between her legs. It had been like this before, only now it was more so. Seven years more.

He broke the kiss and buried his face against her neck, breathing as though he'd outrun a lion. "Nia."

He said nothing more, simply her name, but the sound of it shivered through her like a promise. She scraped her teeth along the point of his shoulder, where an old scar slashed across skin tanned from one too many assignments in torrid climates. His shirt hung half-off, affording her tantalizing access, frustrating barriers.

His hands shaped her waist and skimmed over the slight dip where the surgeons had removed a rib, though he didn't know that. His palms slid up to cup her breasts through the fabric and she moaned.

"Nia?" Logan's voice intruded from without. "Are you okay in there?"

"Just give me one more minute, Logan!"

Then she turned back to Rathe. "I've got to go," she whispered against the side of his neck.

"No. Stay."

"But you just agreed—"

He silenced her with a kiss, tongue delving deep into her mouth, into her heart. Sensation layered upon sensation as he dragged a thumb across one nipple and almost brought her to her knees. "I changed my mind—stay."

She could send Logan away, plead a headache, fatigue, anything to make him go. The bed was a few short paces down the hall. The couch only a couple of feet. The floor nearer still.

As though sensing her acquiescence, Rathe cupped her buttocks and drew her forward and up, aligning the strip of wet silk between her legs with the hard length of his erection. The sensation was intense, incredible, and Nia hooked a leg around his waist, inviting, agreeing.

He slid a hand from her hip to her knee, beneath the dress, and murmured his approval when his fingers found the garter belt and the bare flesh above. "Stay with me," he whispered. "I don't think I could handle it if anything happened to you."

And reality hit with a jab of pain and an ice-cold wash of shame. Maria. This was about Maria.

Abruptly, the heat cooled.

"Damn it!" She wrenched away from him, heart thundering, eyes stinging. She kept her voice low, acutely aware that her "date" still lingered in the hall. "Is that what this is about?"

"I beg your pardon?" Shirt half-off, hair disheveled, pupils dilated to dark pools of sensuality, Rathe still managed to evoke an air of command with the question.

But she was having none of it. "This." She flipped a hand between the two of them and hoped he didn't see her fingers tremble. "You. Me. Maria."

"Maria?" He looked honestly confused, but it was an act. Any man who could morph from janitor to warrior in an instant would have the befuddled routine down pat.

Understanding dawned, and anger sparked in his eyes. "Do you honestly think—"

"That you would seduce me to keep me out of danger? Absolutely." He might not even intend it as such, but the sacrifice could help ease his guilt over her father. Over Maria. Nia was having none of it, though her body still zinged from his touch and ached for fulfillment.

Well, she'd been unfulfilled for more months than she wanted to count. She'd survive a few more. But her career—and her self respect—wouldn't survive if she succumbed to Rathe's blatant manipulation.

He swiped the back of his hand across his lips. "Damn it, Nia—"

"No." She held up a hand. "No more. I'm going to do my job now. You can follow if you like. Or you can go to hell for all I care."

Though the lie tugged at her, she thought it an excellent exit line. She grabbed her wrap and purse, sailed to the door and slammed it behind her. Then she forced herself to smile up at Logan Hart, who was handsome in a tux and tie, and grumpy looking from the wait. She offered her arm. "Shall we go?"

He narrowed his eyes and glanced from her to the door and back. "You're flushed. And I heard voices."

"I took a nap and overslept. Then I had to rush to get ready." She turned away and set off down the hall, forcing him to accompany her and putting distance between her and Rathe. His taste lingered on her tongue, but she knew she'd been right. He wanted her, yes.

But he wanted her as a female who fit into his narrowly defined roles, not as a lover or a partner.

Certainly not as both.

"And the voices?"

She shrugged and draped the dark wrap around her shoulders, forcing herself not to shiver when he helped and his fingers lingered on her bare neck. "The television."

"I see." His dark eyes expressionless, Logan took her elbow and ushered her into the elevator. When the doors slid shut, trapping her in the small space with the physically imposing doctor, Rathe's words whispered in her mind.

Black market organs.

"Everything okay?" Logan's voice echoed oddly, and Nia jolted.

"Fine." She focused on him, on her job, and forced a shaky laugh. "It's been a crazy few days."

"Of course." He glanced at his watch. "If you're not in the mood for this awards deal, if you'd rather not have to think about the case for a few hours, we could go somewhere quiet. Private."

His eyes telegraphed messages that her mind refused to interpret. For the first time she began to feel as though she was in this case way over her head.

And sinking fast.

She shook her head and forced a smile. "No, this is fine. I've been looking forward to seeing Director Talbot at the awards ceremony. I'd rather attend."

His lips quirked. "Of course you would."

"OVERSENSITIVE, HEADSTRONG, hypercritical, suspicious twit." Rathe drummed his fingertips against the steering wheel, mostly to rid them of the tingling memory of the soft skin above Nia's stockings. "You want to go out with our main suspect? Fine. But don't expect me to keep saving your butt."

Despite his words, he parked Nia's Jetta around the corner from the hotel where the awards ceremony was being held, and slipped through a side door. From the wings beside the presentation stage, he scanned the ballroom and saw her immediately.

Dark head bent to catch the words of an older, slightly rounder woman, Nia stood out from the crowd. Wearing a little black dress in a sea of such dresses, she couldn't have gone unnoticed if she'd tried. When she tossed back her head and laughed, Rathe heard it as though she was standing beside him. And when she turned and accepted a flute of champagne from Logan, jealousy and anger knifed in his gut.

"She can take care of herself. Do your damn job." But Rathe couldn't seem to make his feet move.

Finally he yanked his phone from his pocket, dialed her matching cell and buzzed her with the prearranged signal. Two rings, then a hang up. He saw her jolt slightly and wondered where she'd put the phone.

Whether she'd set it to vibrate, as he had.

Whether her body still revved from their kisses, as his did.

With a word to Logan, and the woman Rathe now

recognized as Nurse Marissa Doyle, Nia excused herself and disappeared. A moment later his phone buzzed.

He answered. "What is it?"

"You called me." She sounded annoyed with him, but that was fine. Annoyed was better than in trouble. "Where are you?"

"Around." He didn't want to admit he was watching her. Didn't want to have the conversation that began, *If I were a man, you wouldn't be watching me. You'd be searching Hart's office.* It was true, but it wasn't just because she was a woman.

It was because she was Nia.

Silence hummed across the connection. She wasn't giving him an inch. Finally he sighed. "Stay with Marissa as much as you can. Don't go off with him alone. Buzz me before you leave. Got it?"

"I've got it. I'm not an idiot." Was that pure temper in her voice, or was there a layer of hurt, as well? He couldn't tell. Wasn't sure he wanted to know.

"Fine. I'll talk to you later, then."

He moved to shut the phone, but the hesitation in her voice stopped him. "Rathe?"

He paused. "Yeah?"

"Be careful."

Those two words were almost enough to propel him back in time, to the years when Tony, his wife and daughter had cared for him, cared whether he lived or died.

His fingers tightened on the small, high-tech handset. "Yeah. You, too."

Then he hung up, because what more was there to say?

He watched her return to the ballroom and he grimaced when Hart handed her another flute of champagne. "Go easy on that, honey," he murmured, but knew it wasn't necessary.

Nia French was all about the job.

So he turned away and jogged down the stairs to the street level. He'd search Hart's office first. The janitor's outfit would camouflage him well enough for casual eyes. And Nia…he'd have to trust her to stay in populated, well-lit, safe areas.

Knowing her, he almost turned back.

"No. Get in the car and go. Just go," he told himself, deliberately pushing through the doors and trying to ignore the sour feeling in his gut. The pavement was rain wet and smelled of city—a cloying mélange that varied from place to place but was always underpinned by the smell of rubber, car fumes and humanity.

The funk turned Rathe's stomach. He reached for the car door and jolted as his instincts flared to life.

Nia! She was in danger. He was sure of it. He spun and took two running steps towards the hotel, when a dark figure detached itself from the deep shadows in an alley. A streetlight picked out the sharp angles of the man's colorless face, the corpselike hang of his skin and the bandages neatly wrapped around both hands, where he'd burned them on the incinerator. "The boss wants to see you."

Rathe froze, knowing his instincts had been correct, though moments too late. He and Nia were both in danger. He held his hands away from his sides and eased back a step, away from Cadaver Man. "Thanks, but no thanks. I know what happened to the last guy who 'saw' your boss."

Rathe had to get away. Had to get to Nia.

Cadaver Man frowned, then his face cleared and he snorted. "That what the cops think about Grimsby's eyeballs? Give me a break. That'd be a waste." He glanced both ways, saw that they were alone and pulled a snub-nosed revolver from the small of his back. "We can do this the easy way or the hard way—you choose."

A hint of movement warned Rathe, but too late. Meaty arms grabbed him from behind. He struggled and lashed out with a back kick, but his heel glanced off the huge man with little effect. He choked on the smell of rank, sour sweat, then choked harder when the moving mountain scissored a forearm across his throat.

Cadaver Man watched the proceedings with a faint half smile on his droopy face.

"What—" Rathe forced the words past his narrowed windpipe "—what happened to 'easy or hard'?"

"Why, Dr. McKay." Cadaver Man's face loomed suddenly large in Rathe's vision. He lifted the revolver. "This *is* the easy way."

And he struck the pistol across Rathe's temple. His cheek. His jaw. Not hard enough to break bones. The goal here was damage, not death. Pain exploded and turned the world to gray.

Rathe's blood dripped down onto his shirt and spattered the sidewalk as the pistol-whipping continued.

One thought throbbed through his brain. Nia. He had to get to Nia. Had to keep her safe.

He surged toward Cadaver Man, nearly breaking his own neck in the process, and lashed a ferocious kick that met only air. One last blow knocked the world from gray to black, and Rathe sagged. His captor released his grip, and Rathe collapsed to the sidewalk, retching through split, bleeding lips.

He sucked in a lungful of blessed air and tried to roll away. A kick in the ribs stopped him.

"Search him and tie him up. We're meeting the boss in two hours, after this awards thing is over." Cadaver Man's words seemed to come from far away. Much closer were the rough hands that found Rathe's phone and the knife strapped to his ankle, the voice that chuckled darkly when that knife was slid free.

Rathe cracked his eyes open and recognized the mountain of flesh looming over him. "Fancy lawyer got you out, huh?"

"Shaddup." The pockmarked man scowled. Rathe anticipated another kick, maybe the sting of his knife. He got a strip of duct tape across his mouth instead.

Cadaver Man moved into view. "Hurry up and get him into the car. We're not exactly private here."

Rathe kicked at them both, trying to slow them down, attract attention, anything. Pockmark cursed, grabbed his legs and bound his ankles tightly together with a plastic zip tie. He chuckled, twisted Rathe's arms hard behind his back and zipped them together at the wrists.

Almost immediately Rathe felt the prickles of constricted blood flow. Within minutes his hands and feet would be useless.

Damn it! He fanned the anger, needing to keep the panic at bay. But the fear was there, licking around the edges of his fuddled consciousness. Fear for himself. For Nia.

"Into the car." Cadaver Man waved toward the street. "Make sure nobody sees."

But they wouldn't, Rathe knew. The hotel staff was busy with the awards dinner. Passersby would stick to the main road. The alley was safe for Cadaver Man and Pockmark, potentially deadly for Rathe.

He thrashed when Pockmark tried to lift him, and earned a brutal kick in the lower back. Then Pockmark grabbed him by the zip ties, and lifted him by the two thin plastic strips. The ties sliced into Rathe's wrists and ankles, the pain sharper than the sick agony of his face and the duller throb of his ribs and lower back. He was suspended in the air for only a moment.

Then they threw him into the trunk of a dark sedan.

Pockmark's greasy face loomed into view, close enough to bite if it hadn't been for the duct tape. "Have a nice ride, jerk face."

Then his fist sped toward Rathe's left eye.

Blackness.

Chapter Eight

Where the hell was Rathe?

Nia frowned and buzzed him a fourth time. Even if he was focused on his snooping—or even better, had found something important—he should have called her back by now. Unless he couldn't.

The thought tightened her left eyelid. Her chest constricted.

"Ready to go?" Logan's voice broke in, and she palmed the phone before turning toward him. He held up her wrap and arched one brow. "Everything okay?"

"Yes, of course." She presented her back, and he draped the black shawl across her shoulders. His fingers lingered long enough that she felt the warmth of him. It was a surprise, really. He was so cool on the outside.

"Of course everything's okay? Or of course you're ready to go?"

"Both." Nia turned back to her date and expelled a breath. "Sorry. You've been great tonight, and I've been…"

"Distracted," he finished for her, taking her arm. "I know. So let's get out of here."

Stay in public, well-lit areas. Don't get yourself alone with him. Rathe's instructions spooled through her mind, but she couldn't see any way out unless she ditched Logan—who she was supposed to be distracting while Rathe finished his search.

It had been three hours since their last phone contact. Three hours of rubber chicken and mindless small talk with Director Talbot and his third wife, a bitchy bleached blonde named Yvette, whose sharp green eyes had marked Nia as competition. Three hours of trying to draw out Logan, who had remained hidden behind a cool exterior, seeming amused by her subtle probes. Three hours of wondering what Rathe had found. Where he'd gone.

Rathe, where are you?

"Ah. Here's the car." Logan cupped a hand beneath her elbow and motioned toward the low-slung two-seater as the valet hopped out. "Shall we?"

His eyes challenged her, mocked her. The phone remained stubbornly quiet.

Nia lifted her chin. "Absolutely."

But nerves sizzled to life once she was seated in the vehicle. On the way to the dinner, she'd known Rathe was behind them. The small space inside the car hadn't seemed so enclosed then. So confining. Now it was just her and Logan.

They drove in strained silence. A glance showed her that his sharply defined profile was set, hard. His eyes caught and held hers.

The car seemed suddenly smaller.

They rolled to a stop outside the apartment building.

"Well, thank you for a lovely evening." Nia grabbed for the door handle, ready to bolt.

Logan clamped a hand around her upper arm, and she froze, aware of his size and of the heavy muscles beneath his expensive tux. After a moment his hold gentled. "I'm not the guy, Nia."

Panic flared. She dropped her chin and forced a laugh. "What guy, my soul mate? Isn't it a bit premature for either of us to decide—"

"Don't bother." He held up a hand to stop the lie. "It's okay. It makes sense." He ticked the points off on his fingers. "Whoever it is must have access to the sixth floor, had to know about you and McKay, and likely has a good grasp of transplant medicine." He dropped his hand. "But it's not me. You and your *partner* are wasting your time."

She didn't like the emphasis he'd put on the word, nor did she like that he'd seen through their machinations so neatly. He was smart.

And so was their mastermind.

"Dr. McKay and I will be the judge of that, if you don't mind." She opened the door and climbed out, not caring that the graceless action bared flashes of garter and thigh. "Thank you for an interesting evening." One that hadn't ended according to plan.

She was halfway up the brick walkway to the main doors when Logan's voice called her back. "Nia!"

"What?" She turned, but didn't walk closer.

"My patient, Julia. She had a son. He turned fifteen this month." His lips thinned, his cool eyes sparked. "Tell me what I can do to help."

Nia's brain spun. It could be the break they needed. Or they could be inviting the enemy into their camp. She didn't know whether he was friend or foe, and her mind continued to churn on one vital question. Where was Rathe? She needed his input.

Needed to know he was safe.

So she nodded to Logan. "I'll discuss it with Rathe and we'll let you know." She took a step nearer the car. "It'd help if I could take him something. A show of faith." Another step. "You suspect someone, don't you?" His eyes darkened and she persisted. "Who is it?"

The ice crept back into his expression. "Not a suspect. More an observation."

"Tell me."

There was a strange mix of reluctance and anger in Logan's face when he said, "One of the nurses has overseen each of the dead patients." He took a breath. "Five years ago, her brother died of liver failure because he didn't get a transplant in time."

"Who?" The image of a broad, friendly face sprang to mind and Nia shoved it aside. The nurse had *cried* over Julia, damn it. She couldn't be involved.

"Marissa Doyle." The cadence of his voice suggested that there was a deeper connection there. Was there a history between Dr. Hart and his nurse? Was she his scapegoat?

Or was she a killer?

Confused by this new information, concerned by Rathe's absence, Nia nodded. "Fine. We'll look into it. I'll get back to you."

Logan Hart could either be a powerful ally or a horrendous mistake—and her instincts had no vote on which.

No longer compelled to keep her phone in the background, she pulled it out and buzzed Rathe again, not even bothering to wave when Logan pulled away from the curb. She held the phone to her ear, as though the contact would force the connection through.

It rang. And rang.

"Come on, Rathe. Pick up!" She pressed the phone to the side of her head and tried not to think of how they'd left things—but the guilt had been battering at the edges of her mind all night.

What if he hadn't been trying to manipulate her with his kiss? What if he was equally confused by the chemistry that sizzled between them? She thought of how she'd shut the apartment door in his face and thought of the kiss they'd shared. Of the promise of more.

She'd never worried for a partner before, never wondered whether they were safe or hurt. But she'd never been in a situation like this before.

And she'd never before felt for her partner the way she felt for Rathe.

Maria, she suddenly realized. This was how he'd felt for Maria. They'd been lovers. Friends. Partners. And she'd died. The knowledge quashed the quick flare of jealousy.

"Come on, Rathe. Pick up!" She dialed again, though she knew it was futile. "If you don't pick up, I'm going to have to call Wainwright."

A flash of connection arced through her concern. Wainwright. Bingo. The name reminded her of the last round of tinkering he'd done to the HFH phones. He'd added Global Positioning Satellite locators. She should be able to find Rathe's phone with her own.

"Gotcha!" Still standing outside the apartment tower, unconcerned by the darkness because of the nearby doorman and the security guard in the lobby, Nia punched up the phone menu and scrolled to the program they'd called DOC-JAK, a play on the LOJAK stolen-vehicle GPS recovery system.

Then it'd been funny. Now it was anything but. She punched in Rathe's phone number and waited while the screen flashed a test pattern.

Searching.

"Search faster," she muttered.

She half noticed a sleek white taxi pull up to the curb. When nobody emerged, she waved it off, thinking it was offering her a ride.

Searching.

After a moment the driver climbed out of the cab, cursing. He flung open the back door. "Let's go. We're here." The fine hairs on the back of Nia's neck prickled when a groggy-seeming male voice muttered a Russian curse. "Are you sure you don't want to go to the E.R.? Those are some nasty-looking—"

Target Acquired.

Nia slapped the phone shut and shouldered the driver aside. "Rathe!"

"Hi, honey. I'm home." It wasn't the cheesy line

slurred through split lips that drove her back a step. It was the sight of his face.

He'd been brutally beaten. His left eye was swollen nearly shut. A blue-purple hematoma swelled his cheek to grotesque proportions, and his lips were ravaged and scabbed. Along the side of his neck, extending down what she could see of his shoulder, was a vicious bloody stripe of road rash.

The slits of eyes peering through puffy lids looked baffled and unfocused.

"Oh, Rathe." Anguish tightened her chest. They'd played the game wrong, and he'd paid the consequences. Deeper inside her soul, though, was a flicker of relief.

At least he was alive.

"Is he yours?" The cabbie cut a dubious glance from her fancy black dress to Rathe's torn, bloodstained shirt.

"Yes. He's mine. Help me get him inside." She checked him quickly, cursing when she saw that his wrists were crossed with deep gashes, one of which had just barely missed the critical vessels.

"I dunno." The cabby stuck his hands in his pockets. "He's in pretty bad shape, but he wouldn't go to a hospital. Insisted on coming here."

"It's fine. I'm a doctor. Help me with him, please?"

At her beseeching look, the cabby shrugged, grabbed the wounded man by his already-torn shirt and hauled him upright. Rathe muttered a string of vicious curses in a variety of languages but stayed on his feet.

Nia tugged his arm across her shoulders and ignored

the cloying smell of blood and pain. She was used to it. This was no different from any other patient, she told herself, though the fist around her heart and the sick roil in her stomach said otherwise.

This was different. This was Rathe.

"Lady." The cabby shifted and looked uncomfortable. "I need my fare. I know he's hurt. I wouldn't ask otherwise, but it was a long ride."

She dug one-handed in her purse. "How long?"

"He called from the westbound Framingham rest stop."

"He was on the Mass Pike?" Headed west, miles from the city. The fist around her heart squeezed tighter. She glanced at his face, saw a glint of *I'll tell you later* in his slitted gray eyes. "And you picked him up?"

Another cab might have driven by. City taxis knew better than to get in the middle of a bloody mess. But, she realized with another look at the shiny white cab, a suburban driver might not.

He shrugged. "He needed help. And he looked okay, you know? He looked…trustworthy."

Nia looked at the torn, bruised face of her one-time lover and thought she'd never seen anything less trustworthy. But, damn it, she knew exactly what the cabbie meant.

She handed him two hundred dollars, the sum total of her walking-around money. "Thank you."

And those two words, so often used as a meaningless social pleasantry, came straight from her soul.

"That's too much!" He tried to give half back, but she held up a hand.

"You'll need it to clean your car." She didn't look back at the bloodstained seat, but knew the image would stay with her too long.

With the driver's quiet thanks in her ears, Nia hauled Rathe up the brick walkway, across the lobby and into an elevator. She ignored the doorman's gasp and waved off the security guard's questions with a curt, "I'll deal with it."

If only it were that simple.

Rathe didn't speak until she got him into the apartment. He sank down onto the couch with a groan, then looked up at her. "Lock the doors. Call Detective Peters."

She knelt down between his sprawled legs. "In a minute. I want to look at that cut on your wrist. You'll need stitches, and maybe—"

"Nia." He tipped her chin up with a dirty, scraped finger. "I'll be fine. Call the cops. This is part of the job."

But his eyes didn't call her a weak woman or tell her to get off the case. They were weary and pained. And grateful, so grateful that he was alive. Safe.

Or maybe those were her emotions.

"Don't cry." He touched her cheek and lifted the tear away. "Don't."

"I was so worried." Her voice shook on the words, but she forced herself to hold his gaze. "I knew something was wrong. I kept remembering how we'd been fighting stupid fights, and thinking what if—" Her voice broke. "What if you were injured." Dead. Never coming back ever again.

"Nia," he said again, then sighed in defeat. "Come

here." He drew her into his arms, cradled her face against his chest and curled her legs over his so they were wrapped together.

"No." She tried to push away, but he winced wherever she touched. "I don't want to hurt you."

"Then quit squirming," he ordered with something of his normal grouchiness. When she stilled, he rested his cheek in her hair. "Let's just sit for a moment. Then we can call the cops."

His heartbeat was steady beneath her cheek, and the smell of motor oil and blood surrounded her, all but obscuring his natural scent. But there was no mistaking the feel of his arms around her, the thunder of her heart at his touch.

She might have outgrown her crush on her father's best friend, but she'd fallen back in lust with the man he'd become. There was no denying the truths uncovered in those last few minutes, when it had become clear he wasn't answering his phone. She wanted him. She worried about him.

Worst of all, she *liked* him.

His heartbeat slowed; his muscles gradually relaxed. She wasn't sure if he was even still conscious when she said, "I'm sorry about what I said before I left tonight. I know you weren't playing me."

He chuckled, then hissed in pain. Took a breath. "I'm sorry I made you feel that way. I don't know what the hell to do with you, Nia. I don't know what to do with *this*." He squeezed her tighter. "I just know that when I was bouncing around in that trunk, trying to cut through the zip ties with a bent piece of metal, all I could think about was getting back here and making sure you were safe."

Trunk. Zip ties. The images were horrific, nearly freezing the air in her lungs. But there would be time for explanations later. She burrowed closer, trying to avoid the burned place at the side of his throat. Road rash, she'd thought. Now she knew. He'd taken a header out of a moving vehicle on the Mass Pike. Luckily.

If he hadn't, there was no telling where he'd be right now.

"I was frantic." She pressed her lips to an unmarked inch of skin on his neck, not kissing to excite, but rather to heal. "I'd just activated the DOC-JAK locator when the cab pulled up."

He stiffened. "DOC-JAK? Those phones have positioning technology?"

"Yes." She pulled back to look at his face. Beneath the bruises and the swelling, the scrapes and the blood, his expression was suddenly intense. "Why?"

His eyes flashed with triumph. "Call the detectives. The bastards kept my cell."

RATHE GAVE HIS REPORT bare-chested, sitting on the closed lid of the toilet in Nia's apartment. Detectives Sturgeon and Peters crowded the bathroom door taking notes. Nia sat on the side of the tub with his wrist in her lap, carefully sewing him up with supplies she'd taken from her field kit.

No stranger to stitches, Rathe could ignore the tug of the sutures pulling his numbed flesh closed. He could ignore the faint popping noise the needle made when it pierced his skin, and the harsh smell of antiseptic.

But he couldn't ignore the heat of the woman beside him, or the sight of his half-numb hand lying just below her breast. When she leaned over to knot a stitch, her shirt just barely grazed his fingertips.

"Dr. McKay? Are you sure it was the same man?"

There was a faint chuckle in Peters's question, and Rathe wondered how long he'd been staring at Nia's chest. He fixed his attention on the toilet paper dispenser because it hurt too much to turn his head and look up at the detectives. "Positive. Same acne, same smell, same face and voice. It was the guy who jumped Nia the other day." Bastard.

"I thought he was in custody." Nia's breath washed across the sensitive skin of Rathe's inner forearm. Earlier, when he'd held her on the sofa, he'd thought his body too battered for sexual excitement. Apparently, he'd been wrong. Maybe it was the ibuprofen caplets he'd swallowed with a can of cola.

Or maybe it was simply the woman. And what the hell was he going to do about *that?*

"Out on bail." Peters's answer was terse. "He's got deep pockets."

"Or his boss does." Rathe gritted his teeth as Nia bent over him again and her breast touched his tingling fingertips.

"True." Sturgeon glanced down at his notes. "Do you remember anything about the car? Make? Model? Color? Anything?"

So far, DOC-JAK was still searching for the signal. Nia wasn't sure what it meant, and Wainwright had put his techs on the case.

"No. I can't tell you anything about the car except that it was blue." And it'd been going twenty or thirty when he'd bailed out onto the rest-stop exit ramp and prayed Cadaver Man and Pockmark wouldn't notice. He'd scrambled off the road and into a ditch, where he'd hidden and waited for squealing brakes, shouting men. All the while his mind had clamored for him to find Nia. Protect her.

Peters made a note. "Did the men ever call their boss by name?"

"No. Never. They called him 'the boss.'"

They'd been over the evening twice, but Rathe would gladly talk all night if it kept him focused on the job, if it got them a step closer to finding the bastards who'd grabbed him. If it kept him from having to talk to Nia. He wasn't sure what he wanted to say to her anymore, wasn't sure it would come out right if he tried.

Somehow over the past few days she'd gone from being a nuisance to a necessity, from a past mistake to the woman he'd told himself he had to leave behind.

Which left them where?

With him confused as hell and both of them in danger. It was neither the place nor the time for an affair—or even an attraction. He couldn't afford the distraction.

"Okay, all set." She smoothed antiseptic over the spidery line of stitches and the nearby scrapes and gashes. She bound his wrist in an acre or so of gauze, but when she reached for his other hand, Rathe stopped her with a touch.

"Don't bother. If you try to bandage everything that hurts, I'm going to look like a mummy in no time flat."

Her eyes darkened. "I still think we should X-ray those ribs and get you a CAT scan for good luck."

He took her hands. "I'm fine. I promise."

He wasn't fine. Every square inch of his body sang with pain. But it was bearable. The growing feeling in his gut was not. It spoke of danger nearby. Death.

Peters coughed into his hand. "We'll go check on the GPS signal. Maybe our techs have managed to work some miracles."

When they were alone, Rathe rose to his feet and pulled Nia up, as well. They stood chest to chest in the small bathroom, and he was acutely aware that the cops had taken his shirt, hoping fiber evidence could link him to the trunk of the car when they found it. If they found it.

At that moment all that mattered was that he was bare-chested and she was not.

She reached out and traced the boot-size bruise on his side. He caught her hand, pressed her palm over his heart, though he had no idea what he intended the gesture to mean. "Nia, I—"

"We've got the signal!" Excited voices rose in the living room, thumping feet signaled an exodus. "They're out in western Mass and they're not moving."

Nia and Rathe separated just as Peters stuck his head into the bathroom. "We've found your phone. The GPS blip is weak, but it's there."

"We're coming with you." Rathe didn't bother trying to leave Nia behind. If this was the end of her first investigation, she deserved to be in on it.

Peters didn't bother to argue. He simply held out a windbreaker with Police stenciled on the back. "Sorry I don't have a spare shirt for you."

"This'll do. Thanks." The rayon jacket was cool against Rathe's bruises and rasped across the road burn.

He gestured Nia out the bathroom door ahead of him. "Come on, let's do this."

She glanced at him, eyes full of questions. "Thanks, partner."

He nodded. "You're welcome, partner."

But as he followed the others out of the apartment and made sure the door locked behind them, he couldn't quell the low thump of unease in his stomach.

Perhaps it was a mild concussion or heartburn from taking the painkillers on an empty stomach, but he didn't think so. Something wasn't quite right.

There was safety in numbers, he assured himself, as Sturgeon ushered them to a drab sedan. And they were with the cops.

What could possibly go wrong?

Chapter Nine

The GPS signal brought them down the Mass Pike, to the edge of a wide lake forty minutes away from the city. Peters parked behind a string of local cruisers, and Nia saw a row of officers lined up at the water's edge.

"This can't be good."

She started at Rathe's voice. He had dozed most of the trip, or had seemed to. The detectives had kept up a low murmur of conversation as partners normally did, but she'd been too tired to join in. She'd passed the time looking out the window so she wouldn't stare at Rathe's bare chest.

Now, she glanced over. "Let's see what they have before we jump to a diagnosis." She ignored his sour look. "Do you need help getting out of the car?"

"I'm fine."

Which is why he'd paled to sour milk and cursed under his breath when they'd first walked down to the car. Her healer's instincts urged her to help him, but her self-preservation instincts said the opposite. *Stay away from him,* they said, *he'll only hurt you in the end.*

She sighed as she watched him lurch out of the vehicle, stiff and sore. When had everything gotten so complicated? She'd begun this case with one goal in mind, to impress Wainwright and secure a position in the Investigations Division.

And now? She still wanted to solve the case, but it wasn't that simple. She also wanted to stay alive and keep her partner alive. She wanted to hash things out with him so they could go their separate ways with clean consciences when this case was done.

Didn't she?

"You coming?" And there he was, leaning back into the car and holding out a hand. The windbreaker gaped open around his lean torso, and the kaleidoscopic flashes of blue, white and red lights from the emergency vehicles cast his battered face into strange relief.

The boot-size mark along his side had darkened to an ugly purple. Without thinking—or perhaps thinking too much—she reached inside the jacket and touched the taut skin just beneath the bruise. "I still think you should have an X-ray."

He stilled. There was a flash in the one slitted gray eye she could see through battered flesh. "Nia, don't." He grabbed her wrist.

She jerked back. Heat flooded her face and twisted in her stomach. Embarrassment tangled with irritation as she scrambled from the car. "Fine. It's okay for you to kiss me when the mood strikes you, but I touch you and *wham!*" She snapped her fingers. "I'm being unprofessional. Fine. Don't worry. It won't happen again."

She spun and stalked toward a gesturing knot of uniformed men, stopping only when Rathe's voice called her name a second time. "What?"

He waited until she turned back. He spread his hands away from his sides. The flashing strobes darkened the bruises and blood tracks on his face and wrists, picked out the white of his bandages. "I'm sorry."

After a moment her temper cooled. God, she hated it when she overreacted. "Yeah. Me, too." She nodded toward the lake. "Come on, partner. Let's see what these guys found."

It was a dark sedan, half-submerged in the dark, oily looking water.

"Damn it." Nia shoved her hands in her pockets because she wasn't sure what else to do with them. "They left the phone in the car and took off."

"Which leaves us no closer to finding Cadaver Man and Pockmark." Rathe stood stiffly, and his words were slightly slurred from the beating his face had taken.

Nia wished she'd thought to substitute something stronger for the ibuprofen. Something that would've knocked him out and given his body a chance to recover. Otherwise, he'd keep going until he collapsed.

Which didn't seem that far off.

"Tow truck's here!" a voice called from the road, and the crowd of uniformed bodies shifted and shuffled to make way for the vehicle.

She found herself jostled between Rathe and Peters. She turned to the detective. "Is there anyone in the car?"

He shook his head, his attention fixed on the lake,

where two officers waded into the water dragging a hooked cable. "Seems empty. We'll know more once we get it on land."

The sedan was hauled up within ten minutes, and she pressed forward with the officers to see inside, half excited, half afraid. Excited to find a telling clue. Afraid to see something horrible.

She got neither. Aside from Rathe's phone lying on the dashboard, the car was empty.

"That explains the signal." Handling it by the very edges, Rathe flipped the waterproof unit open and glanced at the display. "Water must've distorted the signal. We'll have to tell Wainwright that his DOC-JAK technology has a bug."

"Hand it over." Peters shot Rathe a dirty look for disturbing evidence, took the phone, and bagged it. "You can have it back after it's processed."

"Fine. Pop the trunk, will you? I want to have a look." Rathe sauntered around to the back of the car, but Nia wasn't fooled by his casual air. His shoulders were set, the lines of his body tense.

For the first time, she wondered what it had been like in that trunk, what he'd thought just before he hurled himself out onto the moving pavement.

She shuddered.

Peters opened the driver's door with gloved hands, waited out the gush of water and hit the trunk release. Rathe eased a finger beneath the lid and pushed it up.

This time the gush of water was crimson.

"Whoa, we've got ourselves a DB!" At the young officer's excited shout, the cops closed in and pushed Rathe and Nia out of the way. But she'd seen enough— and she'd probably be seeing the image for a long time to come.

Pockmark's huge body was curled in a near-fetal position, his knees shoved to his chin, and his hands curled around each other with childlike innocence. One forearm bore a gaping bullet wound, and he'd been shot through the eye.

For an instant Nia's mind substituted Pockmark's face with another, lean and elegant, with cropped silver-blond hair. *Rathe.* She spun around, staggered to the edge of the crowd, doubled over and threw up into a clump of brambles.

A bullet whistled directly over her. Gunfire crackled from the opposite side of the road. The young officer who'd been excited to find the dead body, spun, gurgled and went down.

"Gun!" Rathe knocked Nia to the ground with a flying tackle that wrung a groan out of him. "Stay down!"

She wasn't going anywhere. For one, his good, strong weight was pressing her into the ground. For another, she was too damn scared to move.

Another shot. The cops scrambled for the cover of their vehicles and returned fire.

"Over there! The other side of the road!"

Nia hugged the earth and tasted bile and fear.

The lights flashed dizzying strobes of red, blue and white, picking out the cops' movements, their attempts to flank the shooter.

The wounded officer writhed in pain, both hands clutched tightly to his side, grunting as he tried to bite back howls of pain.

"Come on." Rathe shifted off her. "He needs help."

Nia rolled over and saw Rathe crawling toward the wounded man. He looked back and shrugged. "It's what we do."

Surprise shimmered through her, and a strange joy.

Four days earlier he hadn't wanted her down in the hospital basement alone. Now he was inviting her to belly crawl through a firefight. If she weren't so terrified, she would've punched the air in victory. As it was, she had to force herself to move.

Don't chicken out. Not now. Not when he's finally ready to give you a chance.

She forced the fear into a deep, dark corner, along with the image of Rathe's dead, bloated corpse curled in the trunk of a dark-blue sedan. She turned her head, spat out the nasty taste and began to crawl.

The gunfire grew more sporadic, the cops' voices farther away. Still, she anticipated the sting of a bullet as she wormed her way toward the fallen man. Toward Rathe.

"He's gone!" The shout from across the street was small consolation. The gunman had escaped. He could be fleeing the scene at any moment.

Or he could be working his way back around for another try. There was no doubt in Nia's mind that the bullet had been meant for her. But why? What did she know that Cadaver Man—or his boss—feared?

"Help me take this off," Rathe ordered the moment

she reached him. He held out his bandaged wrist. "We'll use it for a pressure pad."

"I'm not sewing you back up," she argued. "The cruisers have first-aid kits."

"Fine. Get one while I keep pressure on."

Nia scrambled to the nearest cruiser and hunkered down, though there was no guarantee a low profile would save her from a bullet. A middle-aged officer crouched beside the rear tire, sweating profusely.

"I need your first-aid kit." When he only stared at her, she snapped, "Now!" The command sent him into motion. A stream of curses bled between his lips and Nia felt a flare of pity. The local rural cops hadn't been prepared for a shootout.

Neither had she.

"Here." He jammed the kit into her hands, then took a deep breath and glanced at his fallen comrade. "What can I do to help?"

"Make sure there's an ambulance on the way. And keep your head down."

She did the same as she scrambled back to Rathe. He was bent over the officer, pressing his bare hands into the man's side and keeping up a steady stream of low, calming conversation. Their eyes were locked.

Nia paused. Over the years she'd seen Rathe as an adventurer and a grieving friend. As a lover and as the man who'd turned her away. More recently she'd seen him as a reluctant mentor and as the HFH superior who had the power to deny her dreams.

But she'd never before seen him as a doctor.

His voice was calming, his actions precise. And his attention was wholly focused on the fallen policeman, willing the patient to fight, to live.

A fist squeezed Nia's chest, the air backed up in her lungs, and her heart cracked in two, letting Rathe in a little farther than she'd intended.

Much farther than was wise.

"I need all the four-by-fours you have." Rathe's eyes snapped to hers. "Nia! Stay with me!"

"Four-by-fours. Right." She pawed through the first-aid kit, then shouldered him aside. "Let me. You shouldn't stress your stitches."

They worked side by side for the next fifteen minutes, stabilizing the young officer as best they could, alternately soothing him and chivvying him to stay awake. The tension level around them decreased by the moment, as the cops trickled back in, all with negative reports.

"Your gunman got away." Peters crouched down beside Rathe. "How is he?"

"Still breathing," Nia replied, "and he's not 'our gunman.' If you'd found him back when—"

"Here's the ambulance." Rathe's voice interrupted, and she bit back the irritation. The lingering fear.

"I'm sorry," she said to the detective, "I know you're trying."

"Not hard enough, apparently." Peters strode away, leaving Nia feeling small and mean. And scared.

They handed the wounded officer over to the paramedics. He was stable enough that they didn't need to ride with him to the local hospital, so they were cleared to return to the apartment.

And do what?

In the back seat of the detective's car, Nia let her head fall back and closed her eyes. They had two bodies. They had the scant information from Rathe's abduction and a car that had been reported stolen two days earlier. And they had a few pieces of charred packaging. That was all.

Logan Hart claimed he was innocent. She almost believed him. He'd also claimed there was a tie to the nurse, Marissa. Nia wasn't sure she believed that. But if not Logan or Marissa, then who was Cadaver Man's inside contact?

"Let it go." Rathe's words seemed to come from faraway, and her sleepy brain acknowledged their worth. As she sagged toward unconsciousness, she barely felt her head nod in his direction. But when his bandaged arm curled around her shoulder and urged her against him, she knew she was safe.

For the moment.

THE FIRST THING that hit Rathe the next morning was the pain. The next was the realization that he wasn't alone in bed. The first wasn't all that unusual. The second was downright strange.

He lay still, tensing as it all came back in a rush. Being grabbed outside the hotel and stuffed in the trunk. Suffocating, straining, near panic when the zip ties proved stubborn. Convinced the car would stop any second and it would be over. Freeing himself and rolling from the moving vehicle, slamming into the road and skidding on his face.

Worrying about Nia the whole time.

I can't do this.

"Do what?"

He hadn't realized he'd spoken aloud. Now, knowing she was awake, as well, he forced his eyes open and turned, gingerly, on his side to face her.

Her hair was tousled, her eyes slumberous. The faint smell of soap and toothpaste still clung to her from hours before, when she'd let them into the apartment and headed straight for the bathroom. Twenty minutes of showering had left her rosy-cheeked and, hopefully, feeling a few degrees distant from the body in the trunk. The gunman on the hill.

"What can't you do?"

"The police are involved all the way now," he answered without answering. "We can leave it to them."

Her eyes darkened; her full lips formed a thin line. "Darn it, Rathe—"

He reached across, sore muscles screaming with the motion, and touched a finger to her lips to stop the words. "This has nothing to do with you being a woman or me being a man." It did, but not in the way she was thinking. "It's about danger, and what HFH can reasonably expect their investigators to endure. We're beyond that point now. I think we should pull back and let the cops sort this out."

She pushed his finger aside, seemingly not caring

that they were lying nose to nose in a warm cocoon of blankets. The night before he'd been too sore and she'd been too tired to care, and together had seemed safer than alone.

Now he was still sore, but even injured, his body knew very well where he was. And who was lying opposite him.

Nia French. The woman who'd haunted his dreams for a long time after he'd sent her away, believing as her father did that she was better off taking another path. The woman whose memory had plagued him again when she'd called him to her father's bedside and he'd refused.

And now? The woman he couldn't imagine not wanting. Whose possible injury—or worse, death—terrified him so much he was willing to do the unthinkable.

Drop an assignment.

She frowned. "The detectives need our help, Rathe. They don't know the hospital, don't know medicine. We do." She sat up, crossing her arms over her breasts when her oversize T-shirt drooped off her shoulder.

So she wasn't unaware of their position, after all.

Emboldened, perhaps foolishly so, Rathe dragged himself up and leaned back against the wooden headboard, gritting his teeth against the stab of pain. The stitches in his wrist were a background complaint compared to the still oozing slices on his other arm and his ankles. The bruises on his torso throbbed with his heartbeat, his face was puffy and tender, and the road rash along his neck and shoulder flared quick insult at his slightest motion.

"I could've been killed last night." He hadn't meant to say it so baldly, but there it was. If he hadn't escaped, he would've been sharing waterlogged space in the trunk with Pockmark—or worse. When Nia flinched, he pressed his advantage. "*You* could've been killed last night."

The whine of the bullet and her doubling over had happened so quickly, for a moment he'd thought she'd been hit.

An echo of terror, of loss, pulsed through his veins. She was important to him. Too damn important to risk herself like that.

She held his eyes. "This is what HFH investigators do."

"No, it's not." He grabbed her ankle, the only part of her he could reach without moving. "This is above and beyond. Jack would agree. He'll pull us out if we both ask." He took a breath. "What do you say, partner?"

Their eyes held for a heartbeat. Two. Then she slowly shook her head. "I can't."

"Please?" He tugged on her ankle, sliding her closer. "Nadia, if you ever—"

"Don't." This time it was her finger on his lips. "Just don't, okay? You don't understand. I have to see this one through." Before he could ask again, before he had fully registered her soft touch, she slid away and stood by the side of the bed.

Her fingers touched the hem of her sleep shirt, and his breath caught. "Nia, I don't think—"

"I'm not going to jump you. I want to show you something." She slid the shirt up over one hip, then higher. Her panties were smooth, soft cotton—the sort she could rinse in a bucket of camp water and wring dry. Above them stretched a neat scar the length of her hand.

She touched the scar. "This is why I can't leave the case."

He stared at the narrow white line for a long moment while his brain supplied the information his consciousness didn't want to accept. Finally he looked up into her eyes, his libido strangled by the guilt. "You donated a kidney to him."

It wasn't a question. The hints all added up.

She nodded and slid the shirt back down, to where it dangled across the tops of her thighs. As though noting her state of undress for the first time, she made a small noise of distress and pulled on last night's jeans before returning to sit cross-legged on the bed, far away from him. Her eyes were shadowed with wariness.

"Wainwright doesn't know, does he?" It wasn't the first of Rathe's thoughts, nor the most important, but it was the least personal question—and therefore the easiest.

And the most complicated. Though human kidneys were basically redundant, and a living donor could pass a normal, healthy life with only one, HFH fieldwork was far from a normal life. Candidates had to pass rigorous physical exams, or else be assigned to less dangerous aspects of the organization.

She lifted her chin. "He knows."

"And he took you, anyway? He must've been desperate." Rathe didn't consider the words or how they might sound. His mind was locked into a replay of the past four days. She'd been in worse danger than he'd ever imagined. One knife stab in her remaining kidney, one bullet, one well-placed kick—

And she'd be dead. Or on dialysis until they found a transplant donor.

He and Tony had originally met at the field hospital because Tony had been wounded and needed a transfusion. The two shared the same rare blood type. And if Nia had been a match for Tony—

The connection clicked.

"You're a rare type." As was he. Rathe leaped from the bed and swayed as his wounds sang a thousand painful songs and his head spun. "Damn it, Nia. How could you risk yourself like that?"

He meant her pursuit of an Investigations position. She took it another way. Her eyes snapped and she sprang off the bed. "It was my choice. Yes, he was dying from the heart condition, but he wasn't ready to die yet. I gave him fourteen more months of life, and you know what? I would've given him the other one if I'd thought it would help."

He stretched out a hand. "Nia, I didn't mean—"

"Of course you didn't." She paced the room with jerky strides. "You probably think you did him a favor by not coming back. But he needed you. He was scared and he needed you."

What about you? Were you scared? Did you need me? The sick feeling he'd been carrying inside flared to nausea.

He closed his eyes, pinched the bridge of his nose and

nearly dropped when the pain grayed his vision. The smaller aches were fading with time and movement, but the larger injuries remained. Damn Cadaver Man. Damn whoever he was working for.

When had this gotten so complicated?

That was easy. The moment he'd opened an airport hotel door and found his best friend's daughter outside. The moment he'd seen how much she'd matured—from brilliant young woman to *the woman*.

"I never should have let you in that hotel door." Because he had, Tony had ordered him away from the family, away from Nia. For her own good. If it hadn't happened that way, Rathe would've been there when Tony got sick.

But he'd opened the door and owned everything that had happened because of it.

Nia didn't pretend to misunderstand. Surprisingly she blushed and crossed her arms over her chest. "No. That was my fault. You were sick and I took advantage of the situation. We both know you wouldn't have touched me if you'd been in your right mind."

"Bull." Rathe crossed to her and slid his hands from her elbows to her shoulders, holding her still, not letting her look away. Forcing her to see the truth in his eyes. "The moment I saw you standing in my doorway, I knew I had to touch you." He touched his sore lips to hers, didn't deepen the kiss, but simply stayed there absorbing the buzz of contact. Knowing she felt it, too. He lifted his lips, but didn't break the half embrace. "Fever or no, I knew exactly what I was doing."

Making love to his best friend's daughter, ten years his junior. Loving her.

"Yet you left. It wasn't enough. *I* wasn't enough." She pushed away from him and stalked to the opposite side of the room.

"You were everything!" Rathe shouted, surprising himself as a backwash of emotion hit him, desires long denied, regrets long ignored. "But Tony was right. You were better off without me. What sort of life would it have been for you, Nia? Would you have waited at home for me to finish assignments, wondering if I would make it back or whether this would be the time I didn't?" God knows, he'd wondered it often enough, though over time the answer had ceased to matter. "Or would you have followed me from country to country, living in a lousy tent with no running water, surviving on biscuits when the food ran out?" He spread his hands. "That's no life for a woman."

"You didn't have the right to decide that for me." She pressed her hands to the windowsill and looked out. "Neither of you did. It was bad enough Dad warned you off…" The sigh seemed to come from the depths of her soul, a tired, depressed sound. "I hated him for that. I was angry with him for a long, long time. Then he got sick and it didn't seem so important anymore. In the end…in the end he understood why I made the choices I did. At least he tried to." She glanced over at him. "But you didn't even try, didn't even give me a chance to explain when I called."

Her shoulders slumped. Rathe would've gone to her, would've embraced her, but she was a room away.

A world away.

"I left because it was the right thing to do. I left because of how much I cared about you and your father." Why couldn't she see the sacrifice for what it had been?

She snorted inelegantly, but her eyes held hurt. "Feel free to tell yourself that bull, but don't waste it on me. You care about the job and yourself, in that order. It's all about you, your feelings, and what's easiest for you, Rathe. It had nothing to do with me or Dad."

A fist of emotion gripped his heart and squeezed. "That's not fair. I left you because it was in your best interest. And I didn't come back to see Tony because I didn't want him to die knowing he'd compromised at the end."

Or so he'd told himself every day since Tony's funeral, when he'd slipped into a back pew, said his goodbyes and left before Nia or her mother saw him.

"No, you did both of those things because they were easier. Because they meant you didn't have to change your life or your opinion." She gripped the windowsill until her fingertips whitened. "Dad was wrong to send you away, but you were equally wrong to go. And you should have come back when he asked you, Rathe. You shouldn't have used that damn promise as an excuse. You should have cared enough. But you didn't."

Silence followed her final word. Neither of them breathed, neither of them moved.

In that quiet, Nia's phone rang.

"Hello?" She didn't look at Rathe as she listened, but he saw her eyes sharpen, her shoulders square. Her chin lifted, like it did before she went into each battle. "Fine. We'll be right there."

She hung up and strode into the bathroom.

"What? What happened?" Rathe tried to reassemble his HFH professionalism, tried to ignore the words still buzzing in his brain.

It wasn't true, couldn't be true. Denying Tony's dying request had been torture, eclipsed only by the devastation he'd felt when he sent Nia away. Those had been the tough decisions. The right decisions.

Hadn't they?

She emerged from the bathroom and tossed a bottle of ibuprofen at him. "Take some. We're needed at the hospital."

"Another death?" he asked as she strode through the room, dragging off her sleep shirt and not seeming to care that she was gloriously half-naked in front of him.

"No." She dug a sheer white bra out of a drawer and yanked a white button-down shirt from the closet. "They've arrested Logan Hart."

Chapter Ten

"There's nothing here." Hours later Nia pushed away from Logan's office computer and blew out a breath.

"Of course not, or he wouldn't have agreed to let us search." Rathe's words were muffled by the half-open closet door. Instead of coats, the tiny space contained stuffed-to-the-brim file cabinets. But nothing incriminating. The police hadn't found anything, and neither had the HFH investigators.

Yet.

"I don't think he's guilty. He brought it up last night, and I have to admit I believed him." To Nia, the awards dinner seemed a lifetime ago. So much had happened since the night before, since even that morning...

She'd rather forget that morning. She wasn't sure where all the emotion had come from, and the sharp sense of disappointment that had pierced her when she'd realized how wrong things had gone between them.

In his work, Rathe was fearless. The superhero she'd always imagined him. But over the past few days she'd realized he took the emotional easy way out. Blaming himself for Maria's death was a crutch. His seeming misogyny was a front. Even his promise to her father was a convenience.

He liked to believe he'd done her a favor by sending her away, but he'd really done it for himself. Leaving her had been the easier option, turning it into the story entitled "The Time Rathe Hadn't Cared Enough."

She hadn't needed her father to tell her the story. She'd lived through it firsthand.

"You can't argue the evidence, Nia." It took her a moment to remember they were discussing Logan Hart, not their relationship.

"I'm not trying to. I'm trying to make it fit." She opened a bottom desk drawer and rifled through it. "The blue sedan was his—they know that because of the VIN number, right? But the plates belonged to a stolen car of the same general description." Which explained why the police hadn't made the connection immediately.

"Right." Rathe closed the closet door and turned his attention to the glossy, wooden bookshelf. He pulled each thick tome off the shelf, flipped through it and returned it to its place.

"So why bother?" Nia turned her attention to Logan's address book, an old-fashioned leather binder. Black, of course. "If Cadaver Man and Pockmark had already stolen the other sedan, why switch plates? Why not use the stolen car?"

She found a card tucked into the back flap of Logan's little black book. In discreet gold lettering, it spelled out the name of a local matchmaking service. Nia raised her eyebrows.

It seemed Assistant Director Hart needed some help in the social department.

Then again, she wasn't exactly a poster child for having a life, either, so perhaps she shouldn't judge. She'd had just two unimpressive-and-almost-not-worth-the-effort affairs since—

"Find something?"

She blushed and tucked the card away. "Nothing relevant. How about you?"

"No. But that's a good question about the car. You got any ideas?" Rathe dropped into the desk chair and pulled the bottle of ibuprofen out of his pocket. By Nia's count, he'd already doubled the daily recommended dose, mute testimony to his pain. She felt a flash of healer's empathy. A moment of womanly desire to soothe.

She banished her urges and the confusion they brought, and focused on the job.

"Well, I can think of two possibilities. One, Logan is innocent and Cadaver Man's boss is trying to set him up." She leaned against the wall, as far away from Rathe as she could get and still be in the same room. "Or two, he's guilty and has reversed the frame, so we'll assume he's innocent."

Rathe looked unconvinced. "I think—"

"Dr. French?" Marissa poked her head through the door. "Can I talk to you for a moment? I— Oh! I'm sorry, Dr. McKay. I didn't see you there. Never mind."

Nia's left eyelid quivered as the woman disappeared. "Logan said something yesterday…" She hesitated, not wanting to sling accusations but needing to know the truth. For the sake of the patients. Her father's memory. Her own fears. "I'm going after her."

He stood and met her at the doorway, crowding her and reminding her that he was physically stronger than she. Or maybe that wasn't his intent. Maybe that was just her body's awareness of him, of his presence and warmth. Maybe it was his scent, spicy and male through the tang of hospital air.

And maybe she needed to get a grip.

"Excuse me." She tried to brush him aside, but he didn't budge.

"Nia. I'm sorry."

And with a woman's intuition, she knew he was talking about their earlier relationship, not the case. *I'm sorry.* Two little words she would've given anything for at one time. Now perhaps too late.

She looked up at him and saw beyond the bruises and scrapes to the man beneath. The man she'd once loved, though she'd barely known him. She'd known enough, or so she'd thought.

"Sorry for what?"

"I'm sorry I didn't come when you called. All other things aside, Tony was my friend and he deserved better."

If he'd apologized for making love to her, or for leaving, Nia could've armored herself or dismissed it. Though part of her had long ago realized that the situation wasn't as simple as she'd wanted it to be, she could still blame him for his choices. But he'd unerringly found the core of her anger.

Being angry for herself was selfish. Being angry for her father was her right.

"Yes. He deserved better. And so did I."

He held her eyes, and for a brief instant she could see confusion, desire…and regret. So much regret.

Or maybe that was a reflection of her own thoughts.

"I was at the funeral."

"I know." She'd sensed him, though at the time had thought it was wishful thinking. "I saw the plant." A single spindly juniper tree left beside his grave the next day. Sad amongst the blooms and fancy arrangements, it had best represented her father—a man who'd rather sink in his roots than venture abroad.

She had planted the tree beside his headstone, knowing it had come from Rathe. Then she'd waited for him to come to her.

He hadn't.

"It wouldn't have been right," he said, as though she'd spoken aloud. "I couldn't drag you into my world."

"No. I dragged myself." She pushed away and reached for the door. "And now I'm going to do my job. You should try doing yours."

He caught her wrist, and the contact shimmered through her like the dawn, though she cursed herself for the weakness. "Nia. I'm sorry. I swear it."

"Fine." She nodded, and damned the tears that suddenly swam in her eyes. "Apology accepted. Now let me go."

She closed Logan's office door behind her, crossed the hallway and pressed her forehead to the cool glass of a picture window while she willed her heartbeat to slow, willed the tears to subside, willed the memories away.

"I'll be darned," she murmured after a moment. "He's right. Men and women can't work together without it getting personal."

Or maybe it was just her and Rathe.

Sighing, she straightened and pushed away from the window. Heartsore or not, she had a job to do.

It took her a half hour to track down Marissa, mostly because everyone she passed in the Transplant Department wanted to stop her and defend Logan Hart—sometimes quite vehemently—as though she'd been solely responsible for his arrest. It bothered Nia to have so many venomous looks directed her way.

And it made her further question Logan's guilt. Thirty character witnesses couldn't all be wrong, could they?

Sure. Especially when not one of them could suggest an alternative suspect. The nurses, doctors and technicians melted away when she asked, more comfortable with confrontation than suspecting one of their own.

She finally cornered the dark-haired nurse in a patient's room. "You wanted to speak with me?"

Marissa nearly dropped the IV bag she'd been changing. Her eyes shot to the door and the hallway beyond, then back to Nia. "Not here."

Excitement thrummed through Nia's veins. This was important. She could feel it. "Where, then?"

The other woman lowered her voice to a near whisper, as though the walls were listening. "Outside. I'll meet you in the doorway of the photo shop across the street in twenty minutes."

"I'll have Dr. McKay with me." When the nurse hesitated, Nia pressed her. "Nine patients have died, Marissa. Two men have been murdered and both Rathe and I have been attacked. I'm not going anywhere without him."

Though she didn't trust him with her heart, she trusted him with her life. He'd proven himself more than capable of protecting her. And if that was all she could depend on him for, then so be it.

Marissa nodded. "Fine. Twenty minutes. Now go, before someone sees you in here!"

But as Nia left the patient's room, the prickling at the nape of her neck told her it was already too late.

"YOU'RE SURE SHE SAID twenty minutes?" Rathe glanced at his watch again, though there was no need. His internal clock said they'd been waiting for more than a half hour.

"Something's wrong." At his side, Nia shifted uncomfortably. They were pressed together in the small inset doorway of the photo shop, huddled out of the rain, as neither had thought to bring a jacket.

When she turned to face him, their bodies bumped intimately. Her scent, moist and exotic, rose from her damp skin, causing Rathe to tense as his mind whirled from their earlier confrontation.

He was no coward, emotional or otherwise. He'd owned his mistakes. Apologized for them. Been forgiven.

So why did he feel even worse than before? His chest ached hollowly, a deeper pain than the surface bangs and bruises, and at odd moments he found himself wishing for…what?

He wasn't even sure anymore.

For so long he'd been sure of his choices, his opinions. Maria's death had shaped so many of his decisions, from choosing partners to taking assignments. He'd told himself it was solely to protect other HFH operatives from meeting the same horrible end she had. But what if that had been, as Nia said, an excuse? What if he'd been using her death as a way to avoid changing, to keep from moving forward?

No. Impossible. He shook his head and shoved the thought aside.

But it lingered, leaving him wondering *What if?*

"Good, you waited." Marissa joined them, pressing close into the small space even though she carried an umbrella. Her eyes flickered to the passing crowd, to the windows of Boston General towering high above the street. "I'm sorry, I had to—" she paused "—I was delayed."

Instinct flared in Rathe's gut, mercifully blunting the emotions as he wondered what had delayed the woman. An emergency at the hospital? Or something more sinister?

"You wanted to talk to us?" Nia's gentle voice soothed the nervous woman. "We can help you. We can keep you safe, if that's what you're worried about."

Something sparked in the nurse's dark brown eyes, then was gone just as quickly. "No. Don't worry about me, I'll be fine." She pulled a folded piece of paper from her pocket. "Here, take this. I found it in Dr. Hart's trash the day Julia died." She pressed it into Rathe's hand and looked directly at him for the first time. "I hope it helps."

She handed him the umbrella, flipped up the collar of her sensible tan raincoat and darted out onto the sidewalk, where she merged with the flowing lunch crowd. Without the umbrella, she was instantly anonymous. Perhaps that had been her goal, Rathe thought.

"Well, that was strange." Nia tugged the paper from his hand. "What do you think made her so late?"

"I think someone got to her." He folded the umbrella and leaned it up against the wall, instincts humming. "I think she's in this up to her neck."

"Her and Hart both." Nia handed him the paper. "Or so someone wants us to think."

He skimmed the printout, which was a list of Transplant Department supplies with check marks next to a number of them—many of which had gone missing. It told them nothing new and seemed more than a little suspect. He paused when he reached the end of the page. "What's with the drugs written in at the bottom?"

The pen was red, the handwriting distinctly feminine, with a downward slant that suggested the writer was left-handed. Like Marissa.

"Recognize them?" Nia said.

Rathe reviewed the short list in his head. FK506. Cyclophosphamide. Prostaglandin. "They're antirejection drugs, aren't they?"

"Exactly." Though her agreement didn't sound one hundred percent sure. "So why did Marissa write them in at the bottom of the page?"

Was it information she'd been told to plant, or was this an addition, something she wasn't supposed to tell them? Rathe suspected the latter, but wasn't sure what to do with the data. His frustration kicked up a notch at how muddy the seemingly simple investigation had become, how complicated his partnership with his trainee was destined to remain.

He scowled and focused on the paper. "They're antibiotics and immune-suppressors designed to fool the body into accepting an organ transplant." He shrugged. "But it beats me why she wrote them in."

"Me, too." Nia frowned. "Shoot. And I thought we'd caught a break." She jerked her chin back toward Boston General. "Come on, let's have the detectives bring her in for questioning."

Rathe nodded. It seemed the next best step.

Farther up the street, almost directly opposite the main hospital entrance, there was a scream. A thud. A squeal of tires and a chorus of horns blaring in discordant harmony.

Rathe's heart kicked with adrenaline.

"Damn it!" He bolted toward the sound, registering the motionless tan lump in the middle of the road, the dark blue sedan speeding away.

Nia reached the woman first and dropped to her knees on the pavement, heedless of the traffic snarled around them and the shouts and beeps of the drivers. "Marissa!"

Rathe slapped for his cell phone, remembered it was gone and grabbed Nia's out of her pocket to call for help. Moments later a pair of E.R. orderlies and the on-call surgeon flew through the side doors pushing a gurney.

Technically they were supposed to wait for an ambulance and paramedics to transport the patient the three hundred yards to the E.R. But Rathe didn't give a damn. He'd called straight to the front desk.

"Sorry." Marissa was barely conscious, her limbs twisted at awkward angles. A thin trickle of blood ran from her mouth, suggesting anything from a bitten tongue to internal injuries.

"It's okay, Marissa." Nia stroked dark hair from the woman's forehead. "We're here. We'll keep you safe."

Rathe's second call went to the detectives. "Peters, get over here right now. And bring an officer. We'll need a guard."

They lifted Marissa to the gurney. The trickle of blood became a river. Before they could wheel her away, she reached out and grabbed Rathe's wrist with surprising strength.

"It's zero—"

And she passed out.

"Take her." He jerked his head at the E.R. staff. "And keep her alive. We're going to need her." They gave him a filthy look, as if to say, *We always do our best to keep our patients alive.* And then they were gone, sucked back into Boston General.

The image gave him pause.

Nia nudged him onto the sidewalk. "What did she say?"

"She said 'zero.'"

"Zero what?"

"Darned if I know." He moved to scrub his hands across his face, then paused, remembering the sore places and the scabs. He let his hands drop to his sides, his chest echoing with defeat. Because of them, a woman was on her way to surgery.

If she hadn't met with them, hadn't given them the information on the folded piece of paper...

"Come on." Nia touched his arm as Detective Peters pulled into the ambulance bay and parked illegally. "Let's see if they've gotten anything useful out of Hart. And we're supposed to meet with that sketch artist to describe Cadaver Man." She touched his arm again, let her fingers linger. "We're close, I feel it."

Yeah, he felt it, too. But he wasn't sure whether they were close to solving the case, or close to self-destructing and taking a number of innocent lives with them.

He feared the latter.

SKETCH ARTIST was something of a misnomer, Nia soon learned. She'd pictured an artsy type with a pile of charcoal and a half-dozen gum erasers. Instead they were introduced to a computer whiz almost two years her junior who stroked his keyboard like it was his lover.

"Eyes?"

"Yes," she answered automatically, then winced at Rathe's snort. "Sorry. Narrow. Pale blue, almost gray." A pair of light-blue eyes appeared on the flat picture of a disembodied head. She frowned and tried to remember the man she'd seen pushing a canvas laundry cart. "Narrower, and tilted down at the edges."

It took them a solid half hour to agree on the composite, during which time Nia relaxed a bit. The police station felt safe. Protected. Peters phoned in to report that Marissa was in critical condition but alive.

She hadn't yet regained consciousness, so they were no closer to understanding what 'zero' meant. Zero gravity? A zero-point-one CC dose of something nasty? What?

"That's him. Or close enough." At her side Rathe nodded and winced. He reached for his pocket and frowned.

"I took them when you weren't looking." Nia touched his cheek with the back of her hand and told herself she was checking for fever. "You're no good to me if you make yourself sick with an ibuprofen overdose."

His sour look was scant thanks, but it was more of a response than she'd gotten from him since the hit-and-run. He'd withdrawn into himself and she wasn't sure how to follow.

Wasn't sure she should try.

"I'll e-mail this around. We'll paper New England with this guy's ugly mug." The sketch artist cracked his knuckles as though anticipating the task.

"Fine." Nia stood. "Tell Detective Peters we'll check in with him in a few hours. We'll be at the apartment until then." She forestalled Rathe's automatic protest with a warning hand. "I need to change your bandage. I put hard work into those stitches and I'm not going to let them infect. Period."

He followed her out onto the street and down half a block to where she'd parked the Jetta. He paused on the passenger side. "Why does it seem that when we're together, you're always taking care of me?"

He might have been aiming for flip, but the question came out faintly surprised.

It was true. At eighteen she'd helped him past Maria's death. At twenty-one she'd nursed him through the fever and probably saved his life. And now? At twenty-eight she just plain cared.

So she ignored the sarcastic, defensive responses that immediately came to mind and went with the truth. "Somebody has to care about you."

The silent drive to the apartment seemed impossibly long, yet over too quickly, because once the door shut behind them, they were alone together.

And something had shifted in the air between them.

"Into the bathroom. Shirt off." She meant the orders to sound professional, but her voice betrayed her, dropping an octave and emerging in a husky breath.

Eyes hooded, he obeyed her command, shrugging out of the garment and sitting on the closed toilet lid.

"Take this." She pressed a stronger painkiller into his palm and tried to ignore the building electricity as she shoehorned herself into the tiny space.

The night before, the setup had seemed practical. Now, after their conversation early that morning, it seemed too enclosed, too intimate. When she kneeled and began to unwrap his wrist, she couldn't avoid skimming his bare torso with her forearm. Aiming for some distance, she sat on the rim of the tub and drew his arm into her lap, but that was no better. His curled fingertips rested a scant inch from the underside of her breasts.

If she leaned forward just so…

"Nia." His voice was a low growl.

She kept her eyes fixed on his wrist, knowing if she looked up and saw desire reflected in his eyes, she was lost. He was wrong for her, all wrong. He didn't respect her as a professional, didn't see her as an equal. And though he'd apologized for his past actions, the facts remained—she couldn't count on him to be there when she needed him. Couldn't trust that he'd ever choose her over the job. Over his own desires.

Yet, foolish woman, weak woman, she still wanted him. More so now, because she'd seen the man beneath the legend's charm.

And she cared for that man.

"Nia." This time he hooked a finger beneath her chin, forced her to look up. But desire wasn't all she saw in his sleepy blue-gray eyes, there was also something else, something less easily defined.

"What?" Her hands worked to rewrap his wrist, but they felt as though they were acting alone. Her whole being was focused on his face, his eyes, and the fear of what he might say.

If he was looking to seduce her, she was already lost.

"You did good today." He shrugged one shoulder and glanced at the mirror above them. "Maybe you were right. Maybe I've let Maria's death influence too many of my opinions. Maybe I'm wrong—maybe women do belong in HFH. God knows you've been a better, more focused investigator than I have so far...." He swayed ever so slightly.

Of course. A quick flood of surprised pleasure kinked to amusement and Nia grinned. "You're stoned."

There was no other explanation for his quick turn-around.

"I'm what? Who?" His beautiful eyes tried to focus, tried to glare. "What did you give me?"

"Something a little stronger than aspirin. Come on, let's get you to bed while you can still stand." She draped his arm over her shoulders and levered him to his feet. His scent surrounded her, buffeted her, and she pressed her cheek to his bare skin for leverage. Or so she told herself.

"I can stand just fine, or at least part of me can," he said with an uncharacteristic leer and grabbed her hand.

If he'd dragged her fingers down to the distinct bulge in his jeans, she would have dropped him and left him in the hall to sleep it off. But he didn't—he simply held her hand and stared at it for a long, befuddled moment.

"Pretty Nadia," he finally said. "I wrote you letters, dozens of them, maybe hundreds. I never mailed them, but I wrote them. And I dreamed of you—day, night, it didn't matter. I couldn't get you out of my mind. Didn't want to."

He stroked the sensitive skin at the inside of her wrist, and she shuddered. "Come on." Her voice was breathy, not her own. "Let's get you to bed so you can sleep it off."

That had been her intention with the painkillers.

She'd wanted to ease his pain and give his body time to heal. Instead it had stripped him of his natural reserve and turned him into someone she'd never met before.

A man who tempted her with his openness.

"Bed, yes." He spun her with a deftness that denied the sedative and pressed her against the wall with the full length of his body. "But not to sleep."

She lifted her hands instinctively and touched bare skin. Her mind screamed a warning, a reminder, but the noise was all but lost in the roar of blood through her veins, the clamor of her heart.

"Rathe—"

"Shh. It's okay. I've got you." He pressed his lips to hers in a fleeting, oh-so-tender caress. "Nia. *My Nia.*"

It was the reverence of those last two words, the sheer masculine possessiveness that drove her beyond reason. She'd always wanted to be his Nia, even when she'd hated him.

With a small noise of acceptance, of excitement, she slid her arms around his neck, drew his head down and kissed the corner of his mouth, where there was a small spot of unbruised flesh.

"Yes, that's it, sweetheart. That's it." He kissed her back, gently, searchingly, as though they had all the time they could want. As though he didn't share the urgency that suddenly speared through her.

He skimmed a hand down her side, trailing his fingers along the edge of her breast and lingering on the hollow where Talbot had removed her rib to get at her donor kidney. Shock wave followed shock wave, dancing through her body, leaving her pulsing with need. She arched into him helplessly, mindlessly, and rubbed herself against the hard ridge of his desire.

Fear fell away, and with it the aches and pains earned over the past few days. Nia was twenty-one again, and trembling with the power of the feelings he unleashed when he touched his lips to her throat.

This was the Rathe she remembered, the man she'd fallen for. Soft, gentle, almost maddeningly slow in his caresses, he was nothing like his daily self.

Rathe McKay the adventurer had become Rathe McKay the man. The lover.

She tugged his head to hers and delighted in the languid play of tongues. The torrent of heat, of lust, mellowed to a giddy glow as they kissed again and again, changing angles, stroking, touching, feeling.

They staggered to the bedroom, reeling between kisses and laughing at each other, at themselves. And then they were on the bed, clothing scattered, Rathe propped above her on an elbow. His eyes glinted silver with lust, his pupils weren't quite even, and his nostrils flared with deep, reaching breaths.

She touched a finger to the point of his cheek, where the skin remained puffy and sore, a jarring reminder of their situation. "Are you sure? We'll still have to work together, you know. It could be awkward."

"Only if we let it be." He caught her hand and pressed a kiss to the center of her palm. "And we won't."

He kissed her lips, deeper than before, and tucked her

body beneath his. When he skimmed both hands down her sides and cupped her buttocks, Nia was lost.

She gave up control, gave up worry. The warm wave surged up between them, binding them together in a hazy, almost unbelievable dream-reality.

The hallway light was still on, the curtains open, but Nia's entire attention was centered on Rathe. She reveled in the slide of skin against skin, the subtle rasp of rough male hair and the spiraling sensations as he kissed her again and again, loving her with only his bruised mouth and slow, devastating caresses.

She wasn't sure when want turned to need, when pleasant anticipation turned to must have, but when it did, she arched against him, inviting entry, demanding it. And when he slid inside her, stretching her, filling her, touching her deep inside, Nia felt tears sting her eyes.

She'd had other lovers after Rathe. But not one of them had completed her like this. Not one.

Then the time for thought was gone, the time for reason—if there had ever been reason—was past. He thrust into her, and she bowed up to meet him, slowly, still slowly as though there was no world beyond the dimly lit room, no pressures or problems.

Only this.

They moved together, the need coiling tighter into an almost painful ball in Nia's center. She twined her arms around Rathe and locked her ankles behind him, beckoning him deeper and deeper still, until it seemed that he touched her core.

Suddenly he paused.

Nia opened her eyes and found him staring down at her. "What?"

"I've dreamed this. I've dreamed you. Are you really here?" She fell into his eyes, and the question seemed to come from far away.

"I'm here." She touched his cheek, and he turned his head into her hand, breaking the connection.

"Good." He dropped his forehead to hers, and his eyes were pinpricks of desire, of need. "I need you. I've always needed you."

The shock of the words, and one final thrust sent her over the edge into a spinning, confusing maelstrom of tension and light. Her inner muscles clenched around him, wringing a strangled groan as he thrust once, twice, then stilled, not even breathing as his seed spilled into her, joining them into one entity.

Two halves of a whole.

Wow.

The curtain of unreality fluttered open for a moment, then closed in again when he rolled to the side and gathered her close, his front to her back, so they were curled together like completion.

"I've always needed you," he whispered again in her ear. Moments later his arm grew heavy on her side, his breathing slowed.

Amazingly, so did hers.

HOURS LATER Nia awoke, shivering, to find that he'd rolled away from her and taken all the blankets with him. The first shock was the cold. The second was an even more frigid dose of memory.

Oh, God. She'd done it again.

Guilt was a quick slap in the face. At twenty-one, she'd convinced herself his fever had broken, he was fine, he knew what he was doing. At twenty-eight, she knew better, but that hadn't stopped her.

She'd drugged Rathe and taken him to bed.

With a low moan she rolled away from him and sat up, at the edge of the mattress. Wetness pooled between her legs and a tug of remembered pleasure brought sharp tears to her eyes as she remembered her token protest. *We'll still have to work together. It could be awkward.*

That didn't even begin to describe it. What would he say when he woke up and realized what they'd done?

Nia glanced down at his face. The sun-cut lines were softer in sleep. He looked younger and relaxed. Satisfied. But would that last into consciousness? Somehow she doubted it. He might desire her, but he didn't want to be involved with her on this level—he'd made that clear.

She forced herself across the room when part of her wanted to crawl beneath the covers and hide.

Snatching up her jeans and a blue-green sweatshirt, she dressed casually, knowing it was after hours at Boston General, and knowing, too, that it no longer mattered that she look like a visiting doctor.

Her cover was blown in every possible way.

I need you. Rathe's whisper and the slow roll of her heart when she'd heard the words followed her into the hallway outside the apartment, where she found an officer lounging near the door.

"No, don't get up." She waved the startled cop back to his seat. "I'll check in with Detective Peters when I reach the hospital. You stay here and keep an eye on Dr. McKay."

"Is something wrong with him?"

Nia shook her head. "He's fine. He's just...not himself right now." The Rathe McKay she knew would never kiss her so gently or admit he needed anyone but himself.

The officer looked unconvinced. "If you say so. I'll let Detective Peters know you're on your way. And, ma'am? Please be careful."

She nodded and turned away, ashamed that tears had flooded her eyes at the thought of Rathe wanting her. Loving her. She'd needed the emotions so badly years ago, and had finally convinced herself it wasn't meant to be.

And now? Even if they'd been approaching an understanding, even if he'd been beginning to accept her as a partner, and perhaps a friend, she'd destroyed those fragile bonds completely. There was no way he'd trust her now. No way he'd let her be his equal in their work.

The elevator doors opened and Nia stepped out into the dimly lit garage. Instantly the skin at her nape prickled and her left eyelid fluttered, squeezing out a tear. The doors slid shut behind her, leaving her alone in the garage.

There was a stealthy slide of sound from a dark corner.

"Hello?" Suddenly this didn't seem like such a good idea. The officer upstairs could have walked her down. Better, he could have escorted her to the hospital. But no, that would have left Rathe unconscious. Unprotected.

The thought of him, of what she'd done, shattered her calm facade.

"Damn it. You want a piece of me?" She fisted her hands at her sides and strode boldly into the darkness. If she'd had a weapon, she would have drawn it then. But she was unarmed. In her haste to escape the deceptive peace of the bedroom, she'd even left her tool kit behind.

Armed only with attitude and a hint of loss, she raised her voice. "You want me? Come and get me!"

She wanted Cadaver Man out in the open, wanted this case over, wanted to be far away from Rathe McKay and the foolish things he made her think and want.

In the corner the noise sounded again, a scurry—or maybe a footstep.

"Show yourself, you coward!" She'd accused Rathe of using Maria to avoid change, but wasn't she just as cowardly? Only a coward would do what she had done, then run away. She stepped toward the noise. "Come on! You want to fight, you bastard? Let's fight!"

A mid-brown rat squealed and streaked away from her. Nia took two running steps after it, wanting to fight something, to hurt something. Then she stopped, knowing it wasn't the rat she was angry with or even Cadaver Man.

It was herself. She'd done it again, made love to a man who didn't love her and never would.

Blindly she yanked open the Jetta's door and sank

into the driver's seat. She put her head on the steering
wheel.

And sobbed.

Chapter Eleven

Rathe awoke feeling better than he had in days. His bumps and bruises were merely background aches, his face felt like a face, and his wrists and ankles had progressed to itching. He'd always been a fast healer, but this was something more.

This was something warm and wonderful and—

In a flash it came back to him, the feeling of haziness, the looseness of his tongue. The things he'd told Nia. The things they'd done together in the night…

Oh, hell.

"Nia!" His shout was born of near panic. He sat bolt upright in bed, heedless of his nakedness but cringing at the thought of her walking through the door. He'd told her he needed her, that he'd dreamed of her for years, that he'd do anything for her.

This is why men and women shouldn't work together, his subconscious supplied, *it always gets personal.*

"Oh, stuff it," he muttered, then raised his voice, guilty panic shifting to something different when she didn't answer right away. "Nia? Nia, are you out there?"

Of course she was still in the apartment. She wouldn't have gone out alone. She was smarter than that. He levered himself out of bed, bent and dragged on his wrinkled bush pants and loose shirt. The clock read four on the dot, the dark time just before morning.

"Nadia?" Stomach churning with a blend of nerves and worry, he gentled his voice and pushed open the bedroom door.

The apartment was empty. She hadn't even left a note.

"Damn it!" He yanked open the apartment door, startling the young cop outside to instant wakefulness. "Where did she go?"

"Boston General. I radioed Detective Peters that she was on her way."

"Did she make it?" When the cop didn't answer right away, Rathe charged out into the hall. *"Did she reach the hospital safely?"*

"Yeah, she's fine." The officer's mouth kicked up at the corner. "Chill. She's been there an hour, and Peters has had a man on her the whole time."

But Rathe barely heard the end of the explanation. He slammed the apartment door behind him, panic morphing to sheer bloody-minded anger in an instant. How dare she take off without talking to him?

"Stubborn." He pulled on his socks and soft-soled boots. "Irresponsible." He grabbed the windbreaker Peters had lent him and snapped it inside out, hiding the four-inch-high letters spelling Police. "Pain in my—"

He paused in the act of scooping his keys from the floor, where they'd fallen in his mad scramble to shed his clothes on the way to the bedroom with Nia, suddenly realizing that he would have to deal with what he'd said the night before. And he'd said a ton—about Maria, about himself, about his feelings for Nia.

And what the hell was he going to do about that?

He didn't want to take all of it back, he realized with a start. Part of him was willing to admit she might have a point about Maria. Going into the jungle with her rebel lover had been Maria's idea, not his. Though he still wished he could have undone the things that had happened, the horror had been blunted by the years, and by better understanding.

He hadn't loved Maria, not really, and she hadn't loved him. If they had been in love, she never would have left and he never would have let her. But she'd gone, perhaps because she'd loved the rebel leader, perhaps simply because she'd wanted to go. And he'd watched her go, angry more because she hadn't listened to him than because she was leaving.

His grief at her death had been genuine, still was. But perhaps some of the decisions he'd made in her name hadn't been. Like leaving Nia. Like staying away when Tony had tried to call him home.

The fear that he'd done it wrong hummed in his chest, and the question of what he could say to Nia now tightened his throat. *I need you,* he'd said. *I've always needed you.*

And though it might be the deep-down, gut-level truth, he sure as hell hadn't meant to tell her. Not yet.

Maybe not ever.

"Sir? Dr. McKay?" The cop's voice filtered in from the hall, putting Rathe on instant alert.

"What is it? What's wrong?" His heart thundered in his ears. *Nia!*

"I'm not sure, but Detective Peters just called to say you're needed at the hospital. Something's happened."

Rathe was out the door in an instant. Whether or not he was comfortable that they'd become lovers again, she was still his partner.

And it was his job to protect her.

"THIS ISN'T QUITE RIGHT." Talking to herself, Nia paced the corridor for the tenth time, counting her steps. She passed the room where they'd found Short Whiny Guy's body and suppressed the image of his blank face and the surgical slice that had been his throat.

The basement echoed with emptiness. After Rathe's abduction and Marissa's hit-and-run, the hospital administrators had agreed to close the floor and outsource the laundry for a few days. The official word was that the level was closed for routine maintenance, but the hospital buzzed with speculation, even at this late hour.

Hospitals this big never slept. Normally it was a comfort. Tonight it was a source of unease. Nia beat back the shiver with an effort and focused on the case.

"We're missing something." The detectives thought they had the mastermind in custody, in the person of Logan Hart. They were sure that when Marissa woke up—and mercifully, her injuries wouldn't be fatal—she would identify her supervisor without hesitation. All that was left for them was to pick up Cadaver Man and pump him for information. The entire case would fall into place after that.

Or so they thought. Nia wasn't convinced. Perhaps because she'd believed Logan's claim of innocence. Perhaps because Marissa's single word didn't fit their hypothesis about a black-market trade in organs.

"Zero," she said aloud as she paced the corridor for the dozenth time. She'd run through all the possibilities twice, and nothing had jumped out at her. But what if it wasn't zero? What if it was something meant by the word zero. She listed alternatives. "Null, nothing, nada, zip, zilch…"

This was getting her nowhere. And, she acknowledged with a grimace, she wasn't focused. Wasn't centered. While the surface of her brain was counting steps and playing with words, the rest of her was thinking of Rathe, about what they'd done together. About what she'd done to him.

"Dr. French?" Nia jolted at the male voice, then forced herself to relax when she saw Francis, the middle-aged officer Peters had asked to accompany her to the basement. Francis grimaced. "Sorry I startled you. The detective just called—you're needed upstairs. The HBC is awake."

HBC. Hit by car. Marissa! The news lightened Nia's mood a degree. "Good. Maybe she can tell us what 'zero' means."

And thank goodness she was awake. Though the E.R. doctors and her own training had reassured Nia, she had worried after seeing the dark-haired nurse, wan and bruised, surrounded by IV bags and monitors. Her chart listed a sister as next of kin, and mentioned a son, a young boy who needed his mother alive.

"Come on." The officer waved to the service elevator. "I'll take you up."

Nia followed him through the hospital, feeling a knot of uneasy excitement build in her stomach, in her chest. It wasn't until she stepped into Marissa's room that she identified the source.

Rathe.

He was propped against the wall with his arms folded across his chest. He stood more easily than before, and the swelling was gone from his face, though the scrapes and bruises remained. The sleep had evidently done him good.

Though she wasn't sure he'd thank her for it.

Her eyes cataloged the minute details, from the sun lines fanning from his gray-blue eyes to the broad sweep of his shoulders. She memorized him, her mind supplying images of his naked torso, his long, lean legs. The feel of him atop her. Inside her. She flushed at the memory and at the warm wet rush between her legs, the insistent pulsing as her body begged for more.

Rathe scowled, and she glanced at his eyes, which were narrowed. Her heart cracked as vague unease crystallized to certainty.

He regretted their lovemaking, resented the things he'd said, the things they'd done.

And frankly, Nia didn't blame him. It had gone

against everything he stood for, everything he'd decided was important in his life.

Marissa's nurse glanced between Nia and Rathe. "She woke up a few minutes ago, but she's dropped back off. I don't know when we'll hear from her again."

Nia glanced at the vaguely familiar honey-haired woman and tried to focus on the job. "Did she say anything?"

She felt a stir behind her as Detective Peters joined the little group.

The nurse nodded fractionally. "She tried, but it wasn't very clear."

"Could it have been 'zero'?" Rathe asked. His voice was casual, but his eyes pinned Nia in place.

"No. Not zero. It sounded more like 'pig,' or maybe 'fig.'"

Zero? Pig? Nia sighed. "She could be alexic—mixing her words up. It may mean nothing to the case. We need her all the way awake."

"So do her sister and sick little boy." The light-haired woman's words were faintly chiding, and Nia flushed harder.

"You're right. I'm sorry, that was thoughtless of me." Was this part of the process of becoming an investigator? Learning to see patients as sources of evidence rather than living, breathing people with families and friends? Learning to work through personal problems as well as professional glitches? If so, she was learning Rathe's lesson too late—she'd already mixed personal and professional too deeply.

Then the nurse's words penetrated and Nia stiffened. "Her son is sick?"

Logan had said she'd lost a brother to organ failure, when a transplant hadn't been found in time.

"That's right. Harry has congenital liver failure. He's twenty-fifth on the list right now."

Bingo. Forgetting their problems for the moment, she glanced at Rathe and lifted an eyebrow. He nodded slightly in agreement. If Marissa had been bribed with a higher spot on the list, or worse, threatened with having her son's name dropped entirely, she might have done just about anything.

Like pass them worthless information rather than telling them what she'd originally intended.

The three drug names echoed through Nia's brain. FK506. Cyclophosphamide. Prostaglandin. They'd been written in, but what did that mean? Were the names deliberate disinformation from Cadaver Man, or were they a hint in Marissa's voice?

"Come on. We need to talk." Rathe touched her arm and Nia jumped. She glanced around and realized the others had left.

No. She wasn't ready to talk to him. Didn't want to. *You can't make me talk!* she almost shouted, then flinched at the banality of it. Of course they would talk—she owed it to him.

But not here. Not in the Transplant Department, where nothing felt safe.

"Downstairs." She jerked her head toward the elevators and he nodded, though there were questions in his eyes.

They didn't speak as they descended to the lobby, switched to the service elevator and rode it down into the depths. When they stepped out into the basement, Rathe paused. "It's quiet."

As a tomb. The usual machine noise was gone, the bustle of unseen workers and the constant sense of motion was absent.

Nia rubbed the back of her neck and told the fine hairs to settle down when she realized they were alone except for a single guard. Detective Peters had seen to it. "The hospital sent the laundry staff home until this is over."

"Sensible." Rathe nodded shortly, his mind clearly elsewhere. "Listen, Nia…"

"Let's walk." Unable to stand still, she struck off down a less familiar corridor, one that paralleled the one she'd paced before. She needed the motion, the sense of freedom. Of not being trapped. The silence itched at her and Rathe's presence at her side grated, inflamed, until she stopped and spun to face him. "Look. I'm sorry. I'm ashamed of myself and don't blame you for being upset."

She saw a flicker of surprise before he blanked his habitually guarded expression. "Why would I be upset?"

"I took advantage of you." She spun away and stalked down the hall, not counting her paces but rather trying to burn off the energy that pulsed through her body at the knowledge that they were alone together and that the subject they had long avoided would be raised.

Their first night together.

He snorted. "That's bull. I—"

"It's not bull." She glanced back, saw that his eyes were gleaming and felt a thrill of atavistic nerves. "Seven years ago you were delirious with fever. Last night you were stoned. I took advantage both times."

He cursed, grabbed her chin and forced her eyes up to his. "Seven years ago you'd spent two days trying to break my fever and finally fell asleep beside me, exhausted. How did I thank you? By taking your virginity. The guilt is mine."

She saw it in his eyes, in the savage line of his jaw and the deep grooves beside his mouth. "No." She shook her head. "Never. I wanted you. I wanted it to be you."

"You had a crush on me, nothing more. I took that and used it and—" He cursed again and turned into a nearby room. Full to the brim with clean white towels, folded sheets and soft stacks of other laundry, it exuded a pristine, fresh scent at odds with the conversation and the exquisite pain on his face. "You were Tony's daughter."

She followed him into the room, and he shut and locked the door behind him. She barely felt the floor beneath her feet. The shock was too great. All these years, she'd been ashamed by the knowledge that she'd taken advantage of his weakened state, his lowered inhibitions and delirium. To learn that he'd felt the same was staggering.

To learn that he still equated her with her father was aggravating. She fired back, "I'll always be his daughter. But I'm also my own person. I'm allowed to make my own decisions. I made a decision back then, and I made one last night. But in both cases, you weren't in any condition to make your own choices."

"Baloney!" He squared off against her in an instant, eyes ablaze with fury. "I knew exactly what I was doing back then, and I sure as hell knew what I was doing last night. I'd do it again in a heartbeat."

At the word *heartbeat,* hers drummed loud in her ears. "But you couldn't have been in your right mind. You said you dreamed…you said you…"

"I said that I've dreamed about you for years. I said I needed you." The words ripped into her heart like bullets, leaving her raw and bleeding. A rueful smile tipped up the corner of his mouth. "I might not have told you without the painkillers loosening my tongue, but I think I would've gotten around to it sooner or later. I'm so bloody tired of trying to fight this."

He lifted a hand. She expected him to trace a gentle finger along her cheek, as he had before. She was braced for that, and for the warmth that would follow. Instead his fingers tangled in her hair and he brought his mouth down on hers with crushing, inciting force.

She wasn't braced for that, or for the explosion that rocked her body at the touch. He bent her back over his arm, and the intimate play of tongue and lips was enough to smash past the tattered remainders of the barriers that had once guarded her heart.

She felt another stack of sheets topple behind her and fell back onto the soft, clean pile, taking him with her. An incongruous hint of perfume, of fabric softener, rose around them, blotting out the scent of damp, the harshness of the institutional cinder block wall beside them, the acoustic ceiling above.

And then she kissed him back, and all rational thought, all sense of their surroundings, vanished on a quick, exciting slide of tongue and the scrape of a palm.

Different. It was different.

Even as her mind grappled with the realization, his hand streaked beneath her shirt to possess her breast. He rolled her nipple between his fingers, mimicking the motion with his tongue, and with the press of his erection between her legs. Desire, pure and near painful, arrowed through her.

Fast. Too fast.

She must have spoken the words aloud. He paused and lifted off her, enough so she could escape if she needed to. "Too fast?"

His voice was tight. Strain was etched in his features. His arms, bare now, though she didn't remember removing his shirt, were corded with strength and trembled slightly from the effort of holding himself away. Or maybe from the effort of holding himself back. There was a wildness in his eyes, a sexual fury she'd never seen before. It should have frightened her.

It thrilled her. Called to something deep inside her, to the thing that had driven her away from her father to far-off lands. Danger. Passion. Adventure. Rathe was all that and more.

"Should I slow down?" He sucked in a great lungful of air, and the motion nestled him more intimately between her legs in a pressure that sent a fury of edgy, spiky need through her. "Should I stop?"

"No." Never. She would die if he did. "But it's…it's different. Hotter."

His eyes flashed. He very deliberately shifted his pelvis away from her. Toward her. Away. Toward. Through layers of clothing, the rhythm was as old as time. But there was no frantic kissing now, no long, sweet caresses, only this, and the insistent pound of blood through her veins. "I know."

She arched up against him mindlessly, yet acutely aware of her actions, of her body. "Why?"

Was it because of the love that chased through her heart, freed by his words? Or their shared experiences of—

His lips curved up in a rare, pure smile. "Because I'm fully conscious. No fever, no drugs. This is me."

Her skin, already so hot, flamed another degree, from embarrassment, perhaps, or interest. "Oh."

"Sometimes I like it slow and easy." He leaned over her, pressing her back into the soft clean sheets, and took her lips in a soft, sweet kiss that reminded her of the night before, of seven years earlier. She curled her arms around his neck and kissed him back, tasting, questing, restless against him. It was lovely, but not enough. Not this time.

"And other times?" She scraped her fingernails down his chest, deliberately inciting, carefully avoiding the dark, angry bruises.

"I like it hard and fast." Instead of suiting action to words, as her body demanded, he pushed himself away and stared down at her. His expression was open, vulnerable, a bit wary, as though he awaited her pleasure. "How do you like it?"

He was asking more than that, she knew. He was asking her to make the choice she hadn't given him. They would become lovers for real, or not at all. So she gave him the truth that was in her heart. "I like it with you. We'll figure out the rest later."

His smile was blinding and boyish, shot through with the charm of the child he might have been had the foster system not closed him off, had HFH not shown him the darkness of humanity. He leaned in to kiss her, to take her into the fast, hard, burning-hot vortex she could feel spinning just beyond them, but she slapped a hand to his hard chest and neatly reversed their positions.

"Fast, eh? I can do fast." She trailed hot, open-mouthed kisses along his flat stomach while her fingers fumbled with his pants. She'd thought to tease him, to draw out their coupling until this new Rathe, the one with the open expression and joyous smile, trembled with wanting her.

But he was already hard and wanting, and she was the one trembling with need. Or maybe they both were.

On an oath, he yanked at her pants. He took her breast in his mouth and she arched against him, still working him free of his clothes. Then they were rolling, tumbling, fumbling with pants and underthings, no time for gentle words and sighs when the flames burst around them and the urgency sang through her blood.

Take me. Take me. The chant was wordless, mindless,

assuaged only when he finally rose above her and thrust home with no preliminaries, none needed, because she was hot and wet and wanting.

There was flash and flame, heat and speed, but through it all was a sense of wonder, of tenderness. She skimmed her hands across his bruises when she wanted to grab. He thrust into her again and again, hard, fast, but when their struggles brought her up against the cool wall, he cushioned her head with a folded sheet.

This was it, Nia thought as her inner muscles grabbed on to him and squeezed. This was what she'd been seeking. Adventure. Passion. Excitement. Danger.

Need.

Then she was slammed by a wave of it all, a flurry of emotion that crested but didn't break. It continued on and on and on. Even beyond the moment Rathe whispered her name and climaxed with such a look of heartbreaking joy on his face that she knew for certain she would never come back from this place.

Never regret what had come before or what would follow.

THE MOMENT STRETCHED into a minute, the minute into five. Eventually reality returned, and Nia started to notice the lumpy sheets tangled beneath her bare shoulders, the pants still twisted around her ankles. She craned her neck and glanced around the room, at the clothes strewn about and the mounds of sheets and towels that had formed a love nest.

Her face burned and new awkwardness tightened her

shoulders. This wasn't what she'd intended at all. She'd figured they would talk, fight, set some ground rules or maybe agree to never touch each other again.

She hadn't planned on them going at each other in a locked laundry room.

Thinking to turn it into a joke, she started to say, *Do you think the laundry people will know what we've been up to?* But instead a plaintive question leaked between her teeth. "What now?"

His eyes darkened and he sat up, dislodging her. She levered herself up, as well, and readjusted her clothes, needing the armor against the sudden chill in the room. Where moments before there had been giggles and gasps and the slap of overheated flesh, now there was an uncomfortable silence.

Finally he said, "Damned if I know." He sighed and ran his fingers through his hair until it stood on end in silvery-blond spikes. "I've been thinking, though."

Nia's heart jolted. "Yes?"

Maybe he was ready to admit he'd been wrong to leave her, wrong not to come back when she'd called. Maybe he wanted to move forward, be partners, lovers, all the things she'd once wanted. But that thought brought her up short.

True, she'd once wanted those things, but what did she want now?

"I've been thinking that maybe you have a point about Maria. Maybe I have been using her death as an excuse for some things." Rathe tugged his shirt on and snapped his pants as though he, too, felt the chill. Or maybe he needed armor of his own. "Maybe I used my promise to Tony for the same purpose. You're right, it wasn't fair of either of us to make your decisions for you."

She heard the reservations in his voice and knew it wasn't that simple, could never be that simple between them. "But?"

He acknowledged her accuracy with a wry grimace. "But excuses or not, it's how I feel. In the foster system, Father Timory taught us boys that it was our job to protect the women. Cherish them. If something happens to you on this case…" He shrugged uncomfortably, as though the shirt pulled too tight across his chest, or maybe his heart.

A lead weight settled in Nia's stomach. "Which leaves us where?"

He looked at her then, with a wealth of regret and hope in his eyes. "In the middle of a dangerous assignment with nothing resolved." He took a breath. "I care for you, Nia."

It wasn't a declaration of undying love, but coming from such a reserved man as Rathe, the words hit her like blows. She sucked in a breath and pressed a hand to her stomach to steady herself. "I…I care for you, too, Rathe."

His eyes darkened further. "Then bow out of the case. Please. I'm afraid something terrible is going to happen to you."

The subtext was clear. *If you care about me, you'll drop the investigation.*

When the words failed to do anything more than

twist her stomach and harden the ball of disappointment already there, Nia knew she'd expected this all along. Their problems had never been about Maria or her father. It had always been their opposing philosophies. "I can't do that, Rathe. What's more, I won't. If you truly cared about me, you'd understand that."

If you truly cared, you'd support me.

His silence was answer enough. There was no middle ground between them, no compromise.

No hope.

Tears prickled in Nia's eyes and she stood, needing to be away from him, away from the room where they'd loved each other so well, yet not enough in the end. She opened the door, stepped out into the hall and was vaguely surprised to see that nothing had changed outside the little room.

All the changes had been internal.

When he didn't call her back, didn't try to convince her she had it all wrong, Nia knew it was well and truly over between them. She stumbled to the end of the hall, fogged in misery—

And stopped dead.

"What is it?" He had followed her, perhaps to give an explanation, perhaps to fight some more, but now he bristled beside her, ready to protect her from an unseen enemy.

His presence might have irritated her, might have wounded her breaking heart, but her mind focused gratefully on a number. "Twenty-six."

"What?"

She paced back down the hall, all the way to the end

and back, Rathe a silent shadow at her side. "This hall-way is twenty-six paces long."

The hallway that ran parallel, where they'd found Short Whiny Guy's body, was only twenty.

Rathe cursed quietly. "Nia, I don't think—"

But she was already running toward the dead end, her sneakers nearly noiseless. She stopped when she reached the end and faced the blank wall. "It's too short. There's something behind it. A room, maybe." Or worse.

"You don't know that." But Rathe checked the edges of the dead end, tested the doors on either side.

"I have a hunch." Her left eyelid ticked in answer. When he didn't argue, she knew he felt the same. Why else had they discovered Cadaver Man lurking near this hallway several times?

Gratefully, she let the information and the thrill of the hunt distract her from what had just happened between them, what would never happen again. She ran her fingers along the wall. Nothing. The back of her neck prickled in warning, but there was nobody behind her. The floor was sealed off, with a police guard near the elevator.

But there was danger here. She could feel it.

Her fingers found the camouflaged pressure pad just as Rathe touched her arm. He said, "I have a bad feel-ing about this. I want you to walk away."

His eyes said so much more. They offered, promised, tempted.

But in the end it wasn't enough. She wanted it all—both lover and career.

"I have the same bad feeling," she agreed, "but I'm not going to quit on my dreams. No matter what." She held out a hand. "Partners?" Lovers. *Compromise*, she wanted to say. *We can work together. We can watch each other's backs. This isn't my father's life to live, it's mine!*

But he didn't take her hand. His lips flattened to a thin, worried line. "Just push the damn button."

Chapter Twelve

As Rathe watched, Nia pressed the button, and a section of wall loosened. A dark crack opened up between the cinder blocks, where a line of trim and a subtle change in paint color had disguised a rectangular outline. It might not have started as a hidden door, but someone had gone to great pains to camouflage the entrance at the end of the hall.

"Well? Open it!" she demanded.

Rathe glanced over his shoulder. The excited gleam in her eyes punched him in the chest. She loved this. Well, hell, so did he, but he didn't love the sick worry in his gut or the rampaging fear that filled his mind with images of Nia shot dead in a leafy jungle or propped up in a storage room with bloody tracks where her eyes used to be.

He'd made it this long without cracking because he'd trained himself not to care too deeply. At least until now.

"Let's get Peters." He drew his hand away from the knob. "The police should go in first."

"Then get him yourself. I'll just have a quick look

around." With an irritated, faintly disappointed glance in his direction, she opened the door. And paused.

Stairs curled down and to the left, looping behind the dead end. Old-fashioned bare bulbs lit the space with an unhealthy yellow glow. A familiar three-rayed symbol was painted on the wall in black and yellow.

"A bomb shelter?" she guessed

Rathe nodded. "Looks like. Must've been forgotten over the years, as the newer wings were built on top of the older building."

"There's no dust. No burned-out bulbs." She descended four steps, then turned back toward him. "Someone uses this place."

Their eyes locked, and all of his planned platitudes fell away. He didn't bother trying to talk her out of the search. He would've failed, anyway. She'd made her choice, picking the job over him. And he probably deserved it.

God knows he'd done the same thing seven years earlier.

After a moment he nodded sharply. "I've got your back."

They descended the long, twisting flight of stairs. Though the narrow space was no darker than the hallway above, the walls pressed in and the shadows seemed long.

"We should go back up and have the officer radio Peters," he said unnecessarily, knowing they wouldn't. The compulsion had snagged them both, the siren call that touched every doctor crazy enough to trade a lucrative practice for HFH fieldwork.

The lure of the unknown.

"There's a door at the bottom," she said, keeping her voice to a near whisper though there was no sense of another human presence. They were alone. Whispering simply seemed appropriate, just as it seemed appropriate for him to stay close behind her, breathing in their mingled scents and wishing things could have been different between them.

He lowered his lips close to her ear and breathed, "Stay to the side, just in case."

She nodded and glanced back at him, eyes dark in her lovely face. Then she swung the unlocked door open in a smooth move and flattened herself against the wall. But no bullets assaulted them. No cadaverous murderer leaped toward them. Nothing happened.

Then a roiling, charnel stench filtered out, and Rathe swallowed a mouthful of bile. "Oh, hell!"

All thoughts of their recent sexual encounter fled in the face of the smell and the sight of the cavernous room.

There was no body, but it had been the scene of a slaughter. The walls were splashed with a macabre Rorschach pattern of rusty stains. Long rivulets streaked down to pool on the floor, dry now, though they had once been warm and wet.

Nia turned away, breathing through her mouth. "Short Whiny Guy was killed here."

"Yes." Rathe stepped into the small, cool room and felt the walls close in, as though he'd stepped out of the open into a dark, ominous cave. He shook off the sensation and glanced around, though there was little to see.

A lone hospital bed and an empty IV stand gave the featureless room a medical feel, though who would keep a patient in the basement? A rolling stool suggested a doctor's office. And the stains on the wall spoke of torture.

"Why did he stash the body so close to the hidden door?" Nia stayed near the stairway. Footprints, he realized, she was trying to preserve the evidence for the cops. Cursing, he backtracked.

"To confuse us, maybe, or because he's arrogant. He didn't think we would find the door." They nearly hadn't.

"Or because he'd stripped the room clean."

Rathe felt it, too, the sense of having just missed the break. They had a crime scene, yes, but that might not help them a great deal with the larger case. Whatever had happened here was long gone.

He ran through the connections in his head, hoping something would jump out. They had a hospital bed in a bomb shelter. A similar bed in an ambulance disguised to look like a laundry van. Missing drugs but no missing organs. Two dead men and a doctor in custody.

But Logan Hart maintained his innocence through a high-priced lawyer, and Cadaver Man was still at large.

"We're missing something." Nia frowned, breaking his train of thought. "There's something here."

Rathe shook his head. "There's nothing here. Let's call Peters, he'll want to see the room." He turned for the door, suddenly hungry for the clean air above, for the slightest scent of fabric softener, which was now inextricably linked to the sensation of making love to Nia.

"You go. I'd rather stay." Seemingly oblivious to the heavy, fetid air, she leaned inside the room.

She didn't offer to phone Peters, didn't offer to go upstairs with him, which told Rathe she wanted time alone. And the hurt at the back of her eyes told him it wasn't just to examine an empty bomb shelter. She wanted to process what had happened between them, to make some decisions.

Hell, he needed the same time. He didn't like how they'd left things, couldn't stand the thought of them going their separate ways after this investigation, but what was the alternative? He couldn't work with the distraction of a woman partner, he sure as hell couldn't be in a relationship with a woman who knowingly endangered her own life, and Nia had no intention of leaving HFH. So where did that leave them?

Nowhere.

He stifled a curse. "Come upstairs with me. It's not safe down here." He held out a hand and willed her to take it, willed her to understand that he'd barely survived Maria's death, and he'd never felt a fraction for her of what he felt for Nia.

The realization gave him pause, but she was already turning away. "There's a cop by the elevators and the whole basement is sealed off. I'm safer down here than I am in the lobby."

The cool dismissal fired his temper, though part of him knew he had no right to be angry with her. Not about this.

"What will it take?" He caught her arm, turned her

until he had her nearly pressed up against the cool wall. "What do I have to do to convince you to give this up? To give us a chance?"

He thought about kissing her, but the snap of temper in her eyes told him that would be a miscalculation. Besides, there was no need to prove they were explosive together. It was the other stuff that had them at an impasse.

"There is no *us*, Rathe, there's you and some image of a woman you have in your head. That's not me. Until you can see that, until you can accept me for who I am, then there's no point."

"I want you. I've always wanted you. Isn't that enough?" He didn't say *need* this time. It was too close to the truth.

When she said nothing, merely looked up at him, he snapped, "What? You want some sort of grand gesture? You want me down on my knees?" He crowded her with his body, felt the answering flare of warmth between them.

She caught his face between her hands, surprising him. "I want you to accept that I'm an HFH field operative, and will be for the foreseeable future. And I want to know that if it came down to it, you'd choose me over the job."

The inherent unfairness of it struck him square in the chest, and he stepped away from her. "Let me get this straight. You want me to choose you over the job, yet you're refusing to do the same for me."

She lifted her chin. "If that's the way you see it."

If there had been tears in her eyes, he might have

kissed them away. If she'd been angry, he could have picked a fight and dispelled some of the awful tension suddenly strung between them. But her eyes were dry and calm, unnerving him.

She meant it. But he was damned if he understood it. As far as he could see, she wanted him to give in on everything, while she gave up nothing. It wasn't fair.

Love is rarely easy, or fair. Rathe started, remembering Tony saying those words in farewell as he'd loaded Rathe, bruised and battered, onto an HFH cargo plane bound overseas. For all that he'd kicked Rathe's ass over his daughter's honor, Tony's hands had been gentle as they'd buckled him in. Even then Nia's father had known Rathe's emotions were true.

Even then he'd known the relationship was doomed to failure. They were too different.

And too alike.

Suddenly he missed Tony with an ache akin to pain, sharper than the dull sadness he'd felt before, when he'd been far away from the family he'd once called his own. He wished his friend had been there to talk to. But he wasn't. He was dead, and Rathe hadn't said goodbye.

"Rathe? What is it?" Though still cool, Nia's eyes were worried now. "What's wrong?" She stepped forward and lifted a hand, but he moved away, suddenly needing some distance, a moment alone to regroup.

"Nothing. I'm fine." He turned for the stairs, followed by the overpowering stench of death. "I'll go find Peters."

She was right, she was safe in the basement with a

guard at the elevators and all the doors locked. And he needed a moment. She'd be there when he returned, and their problems would remain, as well. Neither she nor their differences would disappear simply because he wished it.

He'd tried that already. It hadn't worked. She was still in his heart. Had been all along.

Halfway up the stairs he glanced back to say something more, but she had already turned away and focused on the empty, bloodstained room. Her mind was on the job, as his should be. She didn't look back, didn't look up, and after a moment he turned away and continued up the stairs, followed by a creeping sense of disquiet.

The cop nodded when Rathe reached the elevators. "Everything's calm upstairs. The patient hasn't regained consciousness again."

Zero. Pig. Marissa's words echoed in Rathe's mind, still making no sense, especially when they were combined with a bomb shelter and a disguised laundry truck.

"Dr. French will stay down here while I check in with the detectives." Though the officer could easily radio the crime scene to Peters, Rathe needed the moment alone. He aimed a finger at the young officer. "Nobody gets in here, understand? And if anything happens to her…"

Something must have shown in his face, because instead of bristling at being lectured by a civilian, the officer nodded man-to-man. "I'll watch out for her."

"Yeah, that's what I keep thinking, too," Rathe muttered as he stepped into the service elevator. He rode up alone, or maybe Tony's ghost stood at his side, but he couldn't outdistance the feeling that he should be doing something different.

Couldn't escape the suspicion that things were about to go very wrong.

DOWNSTAIRS, in the bomb shelter beneath the subbasement, Nia leaned on the door frame and shook her head when the bloodstains seemed to take on shape and form. A dead man. A sick woman. A four-legged creature. All drawn in arterial spurts.

But instead of the case, her mind kept returning to Rathe and what had happened between them. Damn it, she wasn't being unfair. She was only asking for the things she'd give in return. Mutual respect. Unconditional love. Partnership. That was fair.

Unfortunately, Rathe didn't see it that way. Though she respected what he'd come from, and what he'd made himself into since those humble beginnings, she hated that he couldn't see her as an equal. As herself. An investigator.

So investigate, already.

Cursing the thick air, and the gut-deep sense that the room had more secrets to reveal, Nia tried to focus into the dim corner behind the hospital bed. Instead she saw Rathe's cool gray eyes, alive with emotion as he asked her to take him on his terms or not at all.

It wasn't that simple. She balled her hands into fists and used them to wipe away the tears she'd been strong enough to hide from him. "Damn it, Rathe."

With the words came another tear, and the realization that it was time to end this. Time to solve the case and tell Wainwright that she would never again work with Rathe McKay. It hurt too much.

The thought drove her into the bomb shelter, past the dried blood and all the way to the hospital bed. Crime-scene investigators be damned, the answer was in the small, dank room. She could practically taste it, just as she could taste Rathe's flavor on her tongue and smell him on her skin.

Cursing, she shook off the thoughts and focused on the bed. It was stripped of linens and bore no unusual marks. The stool was much the same, featureless and unprepossessing. She'd leave those untouched in the hopes that they would yield a print for the detectives. A fiber. A hint as to who was doing this and why.

She crouched, peered into the dimness behind the bed. And saw it.

"Gotcha." She knew she should wait for Peters and his crime-scene technicians, but couldn't stop herself from scooping up the pill container. She held it by the edges and tilted the label to the yellow light. *Cyclophosphamide.*

And just like that, it clicked. Pig. Antirejection drugs. Blood sang in her ears and joy raced through her body. She had it! She knew!

She heard footsteps coming down the stairs and called out, "Rathe, Detective Peters, I've got it. Marissa didn't say 'zero' she said 'xeno'!"

"Very clever, Dr. French."

She whirled at the new voice. Froze when she saw the gun. Betrayal clawed at her throat, panic fled through her veins. "You!"

There was a disappointed "tsk." "Sloppy of you, letting me sneak up on you like this. Not what I expected of a crack HFH operative." A shrug. "Well, no matter. This suits me fine. I would have captured you one way or the other. I have a customer for your remaining kidney." A faint smile. "That's why you're here."

Nia thought of the holes where Short Whiny Guy's eyes had been and gagged on the thick, redolent air. The eyes hadn't been souvenirs, they'd been used for corneal transplants. Then the words *remaining kidney* shut down her brain. "No! You wouldn't!"

"Watch me." Thin lips curved in triumph, the gun jerked toward the exit. "Up the stairs. We're taking a little ride."

It wasn't an ordinary gun, Nia saw. It was a dart gun, likely filled with a quick-acting sedative. If she moved fast enough, planned her attack well enough…

"Come on, move!"

She moved. She had to get out of the bomb shelter, which must have been used for the black market transplants until the HFH investigation had gotten too close. Up the stairs, in the basement hallways, she might have the advantage. She knew the mazelike twists and turns. If she could outrun—

"Don't bother, I'd gun you down before you got three steps." The barrel poked between her shoulder blades. "Don't think the guard is going to help you. He won't be waking up for quite some time. And your partner? My associate will be taking care of him shortly."

Rathe. They were going to kill Rathe.

Numb with shock, fear and the wild belief that she'd find a way to free herself, Nia didn't truly panic until they reached the loading dock. The laundry van was parked outside, its back doors open to reveal the bed within. The stainless steel equipment glittered and the monitor lights glowed menacingly amidst the slight foggy chill inside the cargo hold. The bed was empty. Nia feared it wouldn't be for long.

Her kidney. If they took her kidney, she would have nothing. It would be a long wait for a rare-type transplant at best, a death sentence at worst.

"Get in." The gun poked hard, just above the empty place where one kidney used to be. She remembered Rathe stroking the scar the night before, tenderly, lovingly. She thought of never seeing him again, never fighting with him again, never having one last chance to compromise—or, hell, give him what he wanted so they could be together.

In the end that was the most important thing.

"I said, get in!"

"No!" Nia spun and slapped at the gun, deflecting the first dart high and wide. She kicked and punched, self-defense classes and sheer survival instincts blending into a messy street fighting style of scratching fingernails and pistoning elbows.

"Damn it!" The gun spat again, and the dart whistled harmlessly past her ear. She broke for freedom, thinking if she could just get past the heavy metal door, just get it closed—

Ssst thwap! The next dart buried itself in her arm.

Pain pinched, then flowed with cool...blessed... numbness.

The last thing Nia heard was the *thunk* of her own skull hitting the cement floor and the rattle of the pill bottle falling from her limp, ineffective fingers.

Then there was nothing.

Chapter Thirteen

The elevator doors hissed open, and Rathe stepped out, fuming at the way he'd been forced to leave things with Nia. There had to be a way to make this work. If only she weren't so stubborn....

A tall, gaunt male nurse kept his head down as he pushed a rolling cart of surgical instruments onto the service elevator. Rathe held up a hand. "Sorry, the autoclave is off-limits today. Didn't you hear? They're outsourcing the cleaning until—"

Tall. Gaunt. Surgical cap and mask, though he'd just passed through the lobby where caps and masks were forbidden. *Cadaver Man!*

"Hold it right there!" Rathe lunged into the elevator, one thought pounding in his brain. If the murderer got down into the basement, he'd find Nia. Hurt her. Growling, "You'll have to get through me, first," Rathe swung at the bastard's head.

Cadaver Man ducked the blow and shoved his rolling cart into Rathe. Scalpels flew in an explosion of sharp steel, and Rathe staggered back. The taller man leaped over the fallen cart, kicked Rathe in the stomach, and bolted for the main entrance.

"Oh, no, you don't!" He wasn't getting away this time. Hart was in custody. Cadaver Man was the remaining link. He couldn't be allowed to escape.

Sucking air past a suddenly kinked windpipe, Rathe scrambled to his feet and took off in pursuit. His boots slipped on the polished granite. Security guards boiled out from their kiosk, but they were too far away. They wouldn't reach the doors in time. And if Cadaver Man got out into the pedestrian traffic, he'd be gone in an instant. He'd done it before.

"Not this time, jerk!" Rathe snarled. The fleeing man was fast, but Rathe was furious. He caught up to his prey just outside the main doors, leaped in a suicide tackle and snagged the other man's ankle.

They went down hard on the granite steps. Agony sang through Rathe's body, reawakening all his freshly healed aches, but it was a good pain. It matched the anger in his soul.

"Going somewhere?" He scrambled to his feet and jammed a boot across Cadaver Man's windpipe. "I don't think so." He pressed down and watched the last bit of color leech from the bastard's gray face. "I think you're going to stay right here. First you're going to answer some questions. Then you're going to jail. Or maybe…" Rathe stepped down sharply, the fury within him taking over. "Maybe I'll just kill you."

"McKay. Stand down." Peters's voice intruded, reminding Rathe he was outside Boston General, not deep in a war-torn jungle, where other rules applied.

He hadn't avenged Maria's death personally, hadn't needed to—knowing that the bastard was imprisoned had been enough. But here, with his boot on the life of the man who'd tried to kill Nia, Rathe felt a primal ferocity, a compulsion to just…press…harder.

"McKay!" A weapon clicked near his ear, brooking no argument. "Stand away. Now! This isn't the way. We've got him, and we've got Hart. It's over."

Rathe was suddenly aware of Detective Peters aiming a gun at him, of a dozen hospital security guards and half that many cops standing in a loose circle on the steps of Boston General. Of the way the pedestrians gawked and the fitful sunlight glanced off the skyscrapers and filtered down to the sidewalk below.

Of Cadaver Man's gurgling, rattling breath.

Oh, hell. Rathe eased his boot off the bastard's neck and forced himself to calm down. "Sorry."

The apology was directed at Peters. After a moment the detective nodded. "Understandable." The sun glinted off his wedding band when he gestured to the others. "Get this garbage off the sidewalk and book him. Hart's already told us everything we need to know."

It was a bluff, Rathe knew. The assistant director of the Transplant Department still maintained his innocence.

Cadaver Man spat a curse as the uniforms pulled him to his feet and Mirandized him. "Hart can't tell you a thing, pigs. And my lawyer will have me out in an hour."

"That the same lawyer who popped your acne-scarred friend loose just long enough for you to kill him?" Rathe asked, putting himself in the bastard's sagging face. "I doubt he's going to have much luck getting you the same deal. We have two bodies, a car and enough fingerprints to fill a database."

"That's bull." But unease flickered in the gray eyes, "You've got nothing."

"We've got all we need." Peters waved to the officers, who hustled their prisoner down the steps towards a double-parked cruiser. "Book him. He and Hart can sweat it out together."

Rathe watched them shove Cadaver Man into the car, none too gently. "It's over, then." So why didn't it feel over? He turned to Peters. "By the way, we found where Arnold Grimsby was killed. There's a bomb shelter hidden beneath the laundry."

And Nia was down there with the blood and the smell, still thinking there was no way for them to be together. No compromise. Rathe felt an odd tug in his chest. He needed to get back to her. They couldn't leave things like this between them.

Peters didn't respond to the news of the new crime scene. He stared at the car. "This doesn't feel right. What are we missing?"

"Detective?" One of the uniforms waved him down to the curb. "I think you're going to want to hear this."

Rathe followed, his guts chilling to ice at the sudden sure knowledge that they had indeed missed something.

"I want a deal." In the back seat of the squad car, Cadaver Man stared straight ahead.

Peters shrugged. "We don't need to give you a deal. We have what we need."

"No, you don't." Cadaver Man turned his head. He looked past Peters and fixed his echoing eyes on Rathe. "You don't know anything."

"The D.A. makes deals, not me." Peters leaned into the car. "But if you give me something I can work with now…" He trailed off suggestively.

The bastard's earlier words echoed in Rathe's skull, *Hart can't tell you a thing.*

"It's not Hart." The certainty hit Rathe such a crushing blow he didn't realize at first that he'd said the words aloud, but Cadaver Man's vicious curse was all the confirmation he needed. "It was never Hart."

Nia had believed Logan's innocence, but Rathe hadn't. He'd been too ready to condemn the handsome young doctor who'd kissed her hand and made her smile. But if it wasn't Hart—

The mastermind was still at large. And when Rathe had seen him, Cadaver Man had been on his way down to the laundry level.

To meet with his boss?

Rathe spun and bolted back into the hospital. *Nia!* He had to reach her. Had to warn her. Protect her.

In the atrium, staff and patients alike were gawking at the spilled cart lying half out of the service elevator, and at the police action on the street outside. Rathe charged into the elevator with Peters on his heels. They kicked the cart out into the lobby, and Rathe jammed his finger on the button for the subbasement.

Let her be safe, he prayed, *I'll do anything, just let her be safe.*

The doors opened on the darkened hallways of the subbasement. He wanted to charge down the corridor, shouting Nia's name. An answer, that was all he needed. A couple of words that would tell him she was okay. But his training held him back just as surely as did Peters's hand on his arm.

They needed to move cautiously, just in case.

Rathe stepped out into the dimness and walked cat's-paw quiet, wishing he had a weapon. Wishing he had an army.

"Nothing," he mouthed over his shoulder, and Peters nodded. Weapon drawn, the detective fanned each doorway as they passed it, though the subbasement echoed with desertion. There was no hum of human activity. No sound of movement.

Nothing.

Heedless of caution, of procedure, Rathe ran the last twenty paces, punched the hidden release, and charged down the yellow-lit stairwell with Peters at his heels.

The detective cursed. "Blood."

Dark smears marred the stair treads, and the tang of fresh iron wafted above the smell of old death. Panic howled through Rathe at the thought of Nia down there, filleted, bleeding out, dying because he'd needed a moment alone and stupidly thought she'd be safe with the officer's protection.

The officer who should have met them at the elevators.

"The guard!" Rathe charged down the last few steps, needing to know, dreading to see. "Where is he?"

They skidded into the small room, and had their answer.

"Damn." Peters barked a string of orders into his radio while Rathe checked the cop.

Uniform askew, the officer lay in the corner, a limp jumble of arms and legs. Blood oozed from his scalp and dripped from a large gash on his forearm. A small dart protruded from his right shoulder.

"He's alive." Rathe's body automatically checked the patient while his mind yelled for Nia.

But she wasn't there. The room was empty but for the officer, the hospital bed, the rolling stool and a trail of fresh blood leading to the door.

Peters dropped the radio to his side. "It wasn't Hart. He's still in custody."

Rathe shook his head numbly, eyes fixed on the blood, the answer coming to him as his brain added up the hints, too late. "No. It was Director Talbot all along. And now he's got Nia."

SHE NEEDED TO WAKE UP, but it was difficult. She was warm and comfortable, soothed by the gentle sway of motion and the baseline hum of the vehicle. And she was tired. So tired.

Wake up, Nia. It was her father's voice, or maybe Rathe's. Rathe. She smiled at the thought of him, at the warm memory of their night together, the spikier heat of coming together in the laundry storage room. At the thought that he cared.

The sensation burned its way to her stomach and made her fingers tingle.

Wake up. This time it was a woman's voice. Her own. *Wake up, you're in danger. He's going to hurt you, going to take your—*

Kidney!

Nia gasped and jerked awake, her brain fighting past the clinging layers of drugged stupor. She struggled to sit up and realized she was tied prone. Panic surged and memory returned with a force akin to pain. Talbot. The director of transplant medicine had drugged her. Abducted her. She was in the laundry van.

They were moving. How long had they been driving? How far had they gone? And Rathe. Had Cadaver Man killed him? Was he alive? Dead?

The thought that he might be gone nearly stopped her heart. God. What if they'd come this far only to be separated now?

She forced her eyes open, and immediately blinked against the harsh glare. The interior of the cargo space was bright with artificial light and closed off from the driver's compartment. Who was driving? Talbot? Cadaver Man? Someone else?

She didn't bother wondering what would happen when they reached their destination. She knew. Talbot, who'd transplanted her left kidney into her father five years earlier, would take her right kidney for someone else, just as he'd taken body parts designated for Boston General patients, sold them to the highest bidder, and substituted pig organs in their place.

Xenotransplantation. Animal organs into human bodies. It was sound in theory, but in actual practice the eventual rejection rate was nearly a hundred percent, even when patients were given megadoses of drugs such as the ones on Marissa's list.

It made perfect, horrible sense. The matching donor organs transplanted into the Boston General patients had been switched with human-looking pig organs. Their bodies had rejected the organs after a few days and the patients had died.

Just as Nia would, once both her kidneys were gone—if Talbot even bothered to keep her alive for the operation. Maybe he'd simply take the organ and let her bleed out on the table.

A tear leaked from the corner of her eye as terror mingled with despair.

The humming note changed. The vehicle slowed and then bumped as though leaving the main road. Gravel pinged on the undercarriage. Heart pounding with sudden, fully-awake panic, Nia jerked against the nylon straps that secured her to the bed.

Rathe. She had to contact Rathe. She wasn't in the hospital anymore, he wouldn't know where to look for her. And if she'd ever needed a rescuer, she needed one now.

Fear and adrenaline cleared the final drug cobwebs, leaving the answer in plain sight. Or at least in her pocket. She squirmed and strained, nearly dislocating her shoulder in an attempt to wedge her fingertips into her side pocket. When she touched the edge of her phone, she nearly wept in relief.

Talbot wasn't as smart as he thought he was.

The truck jolted over an uneven dirt road for what seemed like miles, and Nia prayed it would keep jolting as she worked the phone out of her pocket two-fingered. She was sweating. Her arm and hand cramped with effort and fear. If she could just get the phone open and hit speed dial, she could—

The van shuddered and bucked. An IV stand crashed down, smashing the phone from her fingers. The small device hit the floor and slid beneath a high-tech portable heart monitor.

The van stopped.

The sudden silence was deafening. Tears stung Nia's eyes and she strained against her bonds. It couldn't end like this. Couldn't. There were too many things she still had left to do.

Too many things she had left to say to her father's memory. To her mother, whom she'd drawn away from after his death.

And to Rathe, who was worth fighting for, whatever the cost. She had asked him for unconditional surrender, but had she been ready to offer the same?

The answer was simple. No. And she owed him better. Owed herself better. She owed it to both of them to try harder to make it work between them.

Because whether she liked it or not, she loved him. She didn't just love the heroic figure in her father's stories, she loved the grouchy, imperfect man himself.

She loved Rathe McKay.

Even saying the words in her mind brought a gush

of warmth and a shiver of fear. She loved him, and might never see him again.

As if to punctuate that thought a door slammed. Moments later, the back door to the van rattled up, letting in a flood of midafternoon sunlight. They hadn't been driving long, then.

"You're awake." Talbot seemed neither pleased nor displeased that she'd cleared the drug. He climbed into the van, shoved the IV stand aside, and kicked open the latches that secured the hospital bed to the floor.

"You don't have to do this, Talbot. You can let me go and disappear." Nia tried to get his attention, tried to connect with a man she'd once hugged for saving her father's life. "I won't tell anyone. I promise."

But the old doctor stared straight ahead and wouldn't acknowledge her.

There was no sign of Cadaver Man. Puffing with exertion, Talbot collapsed the bed, pushed it to the end of the van and shoved it off. Nia's feet dropped to the ground and for a moment it felt as though she would overbalance and slam to the ground face first with the heavy gurney atop her. But her captor righted the contraption at the last moment and banged her the rest of the way to level ground. She craned her neck and saw a clamshell drive off to one side of a graceful white-sided colonial.

"Where are we?" When he didn't answer, she persisted, "Where are we going? Why are you doing this?"

Her voice trailed upward at the end of the last question. Incipient hysteria pressed at her throat, and her stomach roiled with fear. The scar where her left kidney used to be pulsed thickly with blood and phantom pain.

She took a breath. "Let me go, Talbot." When he didn't respond, she screamed at the top of her lungs, *"Let me go!"*

The sound bounced off the clapboard and brick wall of the high-class house and was deadened by a ring of pine trees. There were no neighboring structures in sight. A pig squealed in the distance.

Talbot frowned. "Shut up or I'll drug you again."

There was no more emotion in the command than if he was ordering a cup of coffee.

"Why are you doing this? Why? You're insane!"

Lips compressed, he pushed the gurney onto a red brick walkway and followed it around to the back of the house, where a sunken area opened into an unkempt courtyard faced by a single door with office hours listed in flaking paint. "I'm not insane. I'm divorced."

He said it as though the last two words explained everything.

Talbot opened the door and wheeled her through a small sitting area to a sterile-smelling treatment room beyond. "This used to be my office, back when I was married to my first wife, Eunice." He pushed the gurney up against the far wall and kicked the wheel locks. "I had to take the job at Boston General when my second wife, Jolie, divorced me. And Yvette?" He scowled, though he didn't look truly angry. "She's just as bad as the others. I'd kill her, but why bother? This last sale will make me enough money to disappear. That's all I want…to disappear."

He stared at the blank wall for a moment, seemingly lost in thought.

"Please," Nia whispered, weak tears trickling from the corners of her eyes to cool on the soft, laundered hospital sheet. "Please let me go."

"I'm sorry, my dear, but I can't do that. You're a rare type, and just the perfect match for this client." He glanced down at her, meeting her eyes for the first time. "Why do you think I requested help from HFH?" He shrugged as if to say, *It's so simple.* "I need your kidney."

Nia was still screaming when a needle prick in her thigh turned out the lights.

"I'M SORRY, SIR. There's no trace of them on this level." The officer spoke to Peters, but his sympathetic glance touched on Rathe.

"Look again," he grated, refusing to believe she was gone without some hint, some clue. "You're cops. Do your job."

Peters touched his shoulder and Rathe shook the other man off. He wasn't looking for sympathy. He was looking for Nia.

"Cadaver Man isn't talking until he gets his deal from your D.A. friend." He prowled the hidden stairwell, where the air seemed thinner now, as though the herd of bodies coming and going over the past fifteen minutes had cleared out some of the smell. "And no matter how fast that happens, we need the information sooner." He spun on Peters. "Damn it, *he's got her.*"

Saying it that way made it seem certain that she was still alive.

"We've checked the old blueprints, sir," an officer called down from up above. "This is the only bomb shelter."

Peters nodded. "Any luck with Talbot's residences?"

"There's just the one, sir, and there's no answer, no vehicle. We're waiting on a warrant."

Which they couldn't get until Cadaver Man—since identified as Carl Semple—worked his deal and named Talbot as the mastermind.

"Damn." Rathe paced back up the stairs, following the blood trail and hoping it came from the guard's head wound, not from Nia. "If they're not in the hospital, and they're not at his place…" He remembered crawling out of a trunk, crashing half-dead onto a Mass Pike on ramp. "West. They're headed west." When Peters shot him a look, Rathe said, "When they took me, they were headed somewhere west of the city. I escaped in Framingham, on the Pike."

Which led to western Mass. New York. Michigan and Ohio, even. Suddenly, the umbilicus of hope that connected him to Nia seemed stretched too thin.

"Sir! Over here!" The excited shout brought them to the loading dock, where one of the hospital security guards had found a pill bottle.

"Cyclophosphamide." Rathe's throat closed on the word, on the knowledge that Nia had been on the dock, that she had tried to leave him a message. That it was too little, too late. "They went out this way." He remembered that first night, when he'd been so staggered to see her that he'd barely registered the van pulling away. "Put out an APB for a laundry van. White. Maybe letters on the sides, I'm not sure. They'll be heading west."

"There'll be a hundred white vans heading west this time of day." Peters cursed. "We need more."

"I know." Rathe kicked the heavily armored door. "If only we had a way to track—" Peters's cell phone rang. The noise sliced into Rathe's brain.

DOC-JAK. The GPS system. If she had her phone, he could trace her.

In an instant Peters was calling for Rathe's HFH phone to be recovered from the evidence room. They had it within ten minutes, were on the Pike in another five.

And as they screamed along, sirens wailing and local forces already en route to the scene, Rathe prayed like he'd never prayed before.

Let her live.

Chapter Fourteen

Nia surfaced faster this time. Her body was elementally aware of the danger and hadn't let her sink too deeply into the drug. Or else Talbot had been sloppy with the dose.

Alone in the treatment room, which held a blend of old general practitioner's posters and new state-of-the-art equipment, she strained to make out the murmured conversation on the other side of the door.

"No, I told you, there are no security problems." Talbot's muffled voice held a hint of irritation. "The location was moved for both our conveniences, that's all." A pause. "Absolutely not. Nothing will be allowed to interfere with the procedure." A loud sigh. "Of course your guards are welcome here, if that's what it takes for you to feel safe. I'll see you in twenty minutes."

Silence. Nia's brain raced. Talbot had been speaking with the patient who'd bought her kidney. The procedure must have been scheduled to take place in the bomb shelter, nearer their source of supplies—but the plans had changed. Twenty minutes. She had twenty minutes before the client arrived with what sounded like a security force. Bodyguards. Armed warriors with one job—to make sure the operation wasn't interrupted.

She had to escape before then.

The door handle turned, giving Nia scant warning. She forced herself limp, closed her eyes and breathed slowly. She couldn't afford another dose of whatever he'd been giving her. The effects were mild and short-lived, but still…

"You sleeping or pretending?" The voice was very close, and Nia tried not to flinch. "Doesn't matter." He didn't bother to check her pupils. "You're not going anywhere, regardless."

Impersonal fingers pulled her shirt from her waist-band, nudged her pants low on her hip, and probed the site where the incision would go. "Don't worry, you won't feel a thing."

He'd promised her the same thing five years earlier. Back then she'd been excited to help her father, scared of how it might change her life. Now she was terrified. And angry.

She ignored the fear and fanned the spark of anger. She'd need it.

"I'll be back, dear. I need to prep the surgical theater." He left her shirt awry, and she heard him move away, heard the door creak before he spoke again. "It may be more difficult to operate without my assistant, but we'll manage, won't we?"

Then the door closed and she was alone. She cracked her eyes open to be sure of it, then opened them all the way.

His assistant must be Cadaver Man, and if he wasn't

present, it meant… Hope bloomed in her chest. It meant Rathe had defeated him.

She knew there could be a dozen other reasons why Talbot was alone, but she grabbed on to that one. Rathe was alive, she could feel it. If he was alive, he was looking for her.

And he'd find her. She was sure of it. But she didn't have much time left.

She glanced at the clock above the door. Fifteen minutes until the client arrived with his security force. She tugged at her bonds and found them tight, stared down at them and knew she'd never be able to break the thin nylon straps. But the sight of her bound hands reminded her of a med school rotation, when she'd seen a patient seize and twist against his restraints, winding up almost upside down on the bed, though the old man's wrists and ankles had been firmly fixed.

And Nia had her plan. It wasn't much of a plan, but it would have to do. But as she set to work, twisting and turning on the narrow gurney, all she could think was *Hurry up, Rathe.*

She was going to need him.

RATHE CLUNG to the door handle and braced his feet on the floor when Peters hooked off the Mass Pike and flew through the fast-lane toll at seventy miles per hour. "Won't this thing go any faster?"

"Not without wings."

"The locals in place yet?" He rubbed a hand across his sternum, trying to ease the ache.

"They have two men watching the place, with another ten on the way."

Rathe knew that, he'd heard the radio squawk. But he needed to say something, do something. Ever since they'd picked up the GPS blip in a semirural section of central Mass, he'd felt as if they were racing the clock—and it was winning.

"She'll be okay," he said, more to himself than Peters. "She's tough. Resourceful. Everything an HFH investigator should be."

Peters said nothing. He reached across the car and clasped Rathe briefly on the shoulder, then focused on his driving.

They turned off the main road onto a maze of narrow, badly paved back roads, gravel pinging when the back tires slid.

"Almost there," Peters said a moment later. "The dirt turnoff is two miles up."

Nia's phone was sending its signal from an old mansion Talbot had once owned. It was now in his first wife's name, though the local cops said she hadn't lived there for years.

Peters cursed when he narrowly missed the dirt road. He jammed on the brakes, backed up and slalomed down the track. Knowing they were near, that Nia was near, sent Rathe's heart into overdrive with a poignant mix of terror and excitement.

They were going to make it. They would be in time, *had* to be in time. Failure was not an option. Rathe had said goodbye to her once before; he wouldn't do it again.

Not if it killed him. And it was in that moment that he realized something terrifying. Something elemental.

He loved her. Worse, he loved her not in spite of her bravery and insistence on working as an HFH operative but because of it.

He loved the woman she was, not the one her father had wanted her to be.

That was when the radio spat to life. "Sir? We have a problem."

Rathe's heart, which had sped up at his epiphany, stuttered and stopped. No, he thought. There was no problem. Everything was going to be fine. It would have to be.

He needed to tell her he loved her.

Peters toggled the reply. "What problem?"

"Sir, a group of armed men just arrived—and they're not ours."

NIA'S SHOULDERS AND HIPS screamed in pain. Her neck was bent back so far she could barely breathe. But when Talbot returned only a few minutes before the others were due, he cursed viciously, and she knew the agony had been worth it.

She feigned unconsciousness, the spinning in her head almost making the sham a reality.

"Damn it, not again." He tugged at her shoulder and tried to roll her back over. "I hate it when they convulse."

She'd been right in her guess. With his Boston General supplies cut off, he'd been using animal sedatives, which could cause seizures in humans. She'd worked her arms and legs into a contorted tangle, mimicking a writhing seizure.

And, most important, she'd forced her right abdomen deep into the gurney. There was no way he could get at her kidney unless—

"Don't think I won't break your arm." Talbot's tone was conversational, his hands rough as he tried to force her onto her back. "I don't have time for this."

Agony screamed through her, and the elbow she'd hooked over her head poked into her windpipe, graying her vision. She gagged and coughed.

"Ah, so you're coming around. Come on then, sweetheart, give me a little help here." Talbot coaxed her arm over her head, though Nia resisted as best she could without admitting she was fully conscious.

Outside, tires crunched on gravel. Car doors slammed in a rat-a-tat volley of company. Lots of it.

"Bugger. They're here." Finally losing patience with untangling her, Talbot pulled the restraints off her right wrist and left ankle. When he deftly flipped her back into position and yanked on her wrist, Nia reached up and grabbed his sparse white hair. She anchored his head and brought her opposite knee up with a vicious *crack* of bone on bone. Talbot groaned and sagged against her, nearly unconscious.

Triumph filled her, tainted with fear. No time. There was no time to lose. Heart pounding, fingers fumbling with haste and drugged weakness, she struggled to unbind her left wrist and right ankle.

Free, she shoved Talbot's groggy weight off her onto

the floor and stood. Her knees gave out and she sagged, catching herself on the gurney.

Damn it. She wasn't as sober as she thought.

"Dr. Talbot? We're here, where should we put Mr. Bronte?"

Nia froze. The voice was unfamiliar, as was the name—but Talbot's scheme was proof positive that money could buy just about anything, including her life.

Another voice answered the first, "Check upstairs, he might be in the main house."

The voices moved off, but she was conscious of a sense of activity outside the little room, as though the place was alive with movement and whispers. It wasn't safe out there.

But it sure as hell wasn't safe in the treatment room, either.

She willed her legs strong, latched on to an image of Rathe outside waiting for her, straightened and crossed the room. Talbot groaned when she passed, but she paid him little heed. She didn't have time to flip the gurney over and tie him to it, though the bastard deserved that and more.

He'd killed innocent people—mothers, fathers, husbands and wives—for money to pay off his debts. What was worse?

Fury spiked inside her and she glared down. "Bastard." Then she turned her back on him, crossed to the door and cracked it so she could look out into the waiting area. It was deserted, but black-clad men moved beyond the windows, gathering around a long, sleek, stretch SUV. A hydraulic lift descended from the side of the vehicle, carrying a wheelchair. In it sat a silver-haired man, maybe sixty, collapsed in on himself as though he'd lost substance from within.

Nia remembered that look. Incredibly, she felt a spurt of pity, quickly quashed by the knowledge that Mr. Bronte, whoever he was, had purchased her kidney—whether or not she could spare it.

She had to get out of the clinic.

Footsteps overhead reminded her of the two speakers who'd gone to look for Talbot. They would return soon. Rathe hadn't come to rescue her, so she would have to rescue herself.

But his absence beat at her, reminding her of Talbot's threat and Cadaver Man's absence. What if Rathe had been hurt? What if he'd been—no, she wouldn't think of that. Not now. Not ever. Rathe was fine. He had to be.

But even through that declaration, grief beat in her chest. Grief that she loved him without reservation, guilt that she'd asked more of him than she'd been willing to give in return.

In the end neither of them had tried hard enough. She wanted another chance, needed another chance to tell him how much he meant to her. How hard she was willing to try to make it work between them.

"Come on, Nia. Time to get moving." Her lips barely shaped the words, but it was enough to propel her across the waiting room. Her heart beat jerkily, so loud she was sure Bronte's private army would hear the cadence and know she had escaped.

But no, they were focused on the old man and on the woods near the house. Half a dozen black-clad men fanned out into the trees, automatic weapons held at the ready. Four remained behind, surrounding the wheel-chair. All had their backs to the house, apparently judging it secure.

Now! Nia eased open the door and slipped out onto the wide patio. Speed and quiet were equally important, but her reflexes were off and she blundered across the open space, tensed for the shout at her discovery, the shot that was sure to follow.

"Don't let her get away!" Talbot's voice rang out from the clinic door. He reeled out onto the patio and pointed at her. "The bitch nearly broke my head!"

Pandemonium erupted. The four guards near the SUV closed ranks around the wheelchair, lifted their weapons and aimed at her. "Freeze, lady! Don't move or we'll shoot!"

Nia dove behind the shelter of an ornate cement planter and hunched down amidst a hail of gunfire. Small, stinging chips deflected from her meager shelter, and from the stone wall behind her.

"Aim for her head!" Talbot shouted, sounding panicked. "Don't hit the kidney!" He waved his hands. "We need her, we need—" A fist-size rock buzzed through the air and hit him on the jaw, dropping him. Shouts and gunfire erupted in the woods behind the house, and a silver-blond-haired warrior ducked down behind a line of shrubbery.

Rathe! He was alive. The knowledge speared through

Nia like a starburst and she cried out when the guards fired blindly into the landscaping. Rhododendrons and azaleas exploded in a hail of bullets, but when the fusillade ended, there was no sign of a body.

"Sorry I'm late." His voice spoke at her shoulder and she whirled, disbelief hammering in her mind, hope blasting through her soul.

"Rathe!"

He caught her in a crushing embrace, and Nia curled into him, needing the contact, the reassurance that he was still alive, that she was, too.

"They're over here! This way!"

The shout broke them apart, but Rathe kept hold of her hand as though he never intended to let go. His energy buzzed through the contact, strengthening her, warming her. He cocked an eyebrow. "Ready, partner?"

She was conscious of the excitement swirling in her stomach, of the black-suited men fanning out along one side of her hiding place, and of the absolute, utter confidence in Rathe's eyes. She nodded. "Ready."

He jerked his chin toward the tree line, where the gunfire had dwindled to sporadic chatter. "Work your way behind the house and back toward the road. Peters has a car there."

"Where will you be?" She lifted her chin, expecting him to put her in her place, to tell her to hide behind the lines, where the women belong.

He surprised her by smiling. "Right behind you." He kissed her quickly. "I love you. Now go!"

Heart thundering from a mix of nerves and joyous excitement at his declaration, she bolted from behind the planter, keeping low beside the stone wall. She heard excited shouts and the stitch of gunfire moving away from her.

She dove behind a long-dry fountain and looked back. "Damn it, *I believed you!*"

Which was her own stupid fault. Of course Rathe had drawn their fire. He was a bloody hero.

Instead of right behind her, he was on the opposite side of the patio, pinned down by two of the guards while the other two hustled to load Bronte back into the stretch SUV. Worse, Talbot was on the move. Hidden by the same planter Nia had crouched behind, the doctor was advancing on Rathe with a wickedly pointed surgical instrument—a trocar—in his hand.

The long, thin, metal blade was designed to create an incision for thin tubing. It could easily pierce a man's heart with a trained jab.

"Rathe, behind you!"

But her shout was lost in a loudspeaker's crackle as Peters's voice called, "Put down your weapons. We have the others in custody and you are surrounded. Put down your weapons, now!"

The guards nearly tossed the wheelchair into the huge vehicle. Two jumped in, fired the engine and sped away, leaving the other two behind to fight a rear-guard action. One sent a spray of bullets towards Peters's voice, the other scowled and aimed at Rathe.

"No!" Nia broke cover and charged across the patio,

hoping to draw the fire, to protect him from Talbot's approach, to warn him at the very least.

Rathe spun. His lips shaped a cry she didn't hear as it was lost amidst a quick volley of gunfire. The two guards were cut down in a spray of bullets. Nia misjudged her footing and went down, crashing into Talbot on the way. They fell together in a tangle, squirming and grappling for the upper hand.

Talbot loomed above her. "You were my ticket out of here, bitch!" A searing pain, cool blue and hot red, cut into Nia's side, and she screamed when Talbot raised the bloody trocar and aimed it at her eye.

"Bastard!" Rathe lifted Talbot bodily off her. The older doctor reeled and swung at Rathe, who danced back and flashed a kick that broke Talbot's kneecap. "She's mine!" He followed the anguished shout with a trained one-two-three combination that would have ended in a killing blow.

But he ended on "two" and stood over his fallen enemy, breathing hard, as uniformed officers in Kevlar vests poured onto the scene.

Nia struggled to her feet and hunched over awkwardly, trying to relieve the pain in her side. She must have fallen on a rock. She sucked in a breath. "Good job, McKay."

Molten silver eyes locked on her, their depths flowing with adrenaline and relief. "You're okay?"

"Fine. I just have a stitch in my side. It'll pass." But it wasn't passing. It was growing worse by the moment. She looked down at Talbot and felt, incredibly, a beat of sadness. "He was a good doctor, once. But he said his ex-wives kept wanting more…."

Rathe's eyes sharpened to flint. "This was his fault, not theirs."

"I know." Nia was suddenly tired. So tired. She sighed shallowly and tried to grin as she scanned the destruction all around them, the scattered bodies and the stretch SUV leaning drunkenly where it had plowed into a police-car roadblock. "Well, my first case is over. Guess this proves your point about women partners being nothing but trouble, huh?"

"No. Exactly the opposite." He reached over and tipped her chin up. "At every turn in this case, you were stronger and more focused than me. We wouldn't have gotten to this point without your skills." He stepped in close. "You're a credit to HFH, and I'd be honored to work with you again."

His kiss told her more, and when their lips parted, he whispered, "I love you. Marry me. We can make this work, I swear it." And he kissed her again.

The world shifted beneath her, lurching as though cosmic forces were realigning themselves below her feet. "I love you too, but I can't…I can't think." She put a hand to her head, trying to block out the roaring, rushing noise. "I can't—"

And the roaring caught her, swamped over her and carried her away on a swirl of chaos. She felt herself fall, felt strong arms catch her and cradle her against a warm, solid chest. She felt a gurney beneath her and struggled when hands tried to strap her down.

"Leave it. I'll hold her."

She turned toward Rathe's voice, saw the panic in his eyes and reached out a hand to soothe. "It's okay, I feel—" Not fine. The sting in her side evolved to a pulsing, sickening throb. The motion of the ambulance and the siren's sob made it worse, and the whispered words fluttered above her.

Nicked the kidney...dialysis...transplant.

The last word shocked her back to awareness. "No!" She tried to sit up, tried to fight the hands that held her down.

"Nia, calm down. It's me. I'm here. You'll be okay." Rathe gripped her hand, and she felt the strength flow between them. "I promise."

The ambulance stopped, the doors opened onto the chaos of an E.R. Another gurney rolled past, and Nia caught a glimpse of white hair, sunken eyes, and pale, drawn skin. "Poor man."

Rathe's hand tightened. "He tried to buy your life from Talbot. There's no need for pity—he'll get what's coming to him, death by kidney failure."

"Nobody deserves to die that way." She thought she said the words aloud, but she was floating away, into another reality, where her side didn't hurt and she could barely feel the pressure of Rathe's fingers on hers.

"Are you McKay?" The new voice was startling, and Nia fought to hold on to Rathe when he pulled away.

"Yes. Where do I go?"

"There's some paperwork first. Jack Wainwright filled out your information, but..." The words trailed off into the haze, but Nia's brain struggled to comprehend as she was wheeled through corridors that were not, thankfully, those of Boston General.

A nurse leaned close. "You're a lucky young woman. What are the odds of your boyfriend being a match?"

And Nia understood. "Get him in here."

"Don't worry, dear. Everything will be fine."

Panic lent strength to Nia's cotton-wool arms. She grabbed the nurse. "Get Rathe in here, *now.*"

He was there in moments, or maybe an hour; her concept of time had spun away along with the rest of her senses. But when she saw his dear face, saw the love shining in his eyes beside the worry, she found the energy to snarl, "Don't you dare."

"Now, Nia—"

"Don't you 'now, Nia' me, buster. Don't do it. I can go on dialysis until they find a match."

"I am your match." He said the words so calmly, with such conviction, that she couldn't speak for a moment. They were the words she'd longed to hear, but not the situation she'd imagined. Not the sacrifice she would have chosen.

And in the moment she hesitated, the drugs kicked in and she was falling…falling…

And he was there to catch her.

A FEW HOURS LATER, she woke up with her mouth nearly dried shut and every cell in her body singing in pain. But it was a good pain, an *alive* pain that told her she'd made it, one way or the other.

She hoped it hadn't been the other. Those last few fuzzy moments replayed in her brain, and guilt thrummed heavily. "He didn't have to do it," she whispered, though her words were nearly lost in the dryness.

"Huh? Whuzzat?" A heavy weight shifted at the edge of the bed.

Nia opened her eyes and found him there beside her. And if he'd been sleeping sitting up at her bedside, then… "They didn't need your kidney." The words came out clearer this time.

His wonderful gray eyes warmed. "Nope. Yours was fixable. It'll be as good as new in a month or so."

Remembering what she thought she'd said, thought she'd overheard, she picked at the sheet.

"What about Marissa? Logan?" They weren't the most important questions, but they were the simpler ones. Easier than asking about them, asking about love.

A gleam in Rathe's eyes chided her for being a coward. "Marissa will be fine, and Wainwright is on the lookout for a liver for her son Harry. We were right, Talbot had used the boy's illness as leverage to force her to give the patients the extra drugs without asking too many questions. He told her it was part of a semiorthodox study he was running. It wasn't until that last death that she realized there was something more going on."

Poor Marissa. Nia felt a beat of pity. "And Logan?"

Rathe stretched, and a host of muscles pressed against his soft black T-shirt. *Her muscles,* Nia thought possessively, and was surprised to feel a slow surge of lust through the pain. He cocked his head, eyes glinting as though he'd read her mind. "Believe it or not, Hart's interviewing with HFH. Said he got a taste of things watching us work and wants to live the adventure—God help him." Lips curving in a sensuous, almost carefree smile, Rathe leaned toward her. "He'll stay here and re-organize the Transplant Department first. We'll leave as soon as you're feeling up to it."

"Oh." Disappointment sang through her like an ache and irritation built like a roar. "Where are you off to, then?" *Don't you dare say on assignment without me, buster.*

He slid her a glance. "Wainwright has a job lined up for us in the Outback."

Us. As in Nia and Rathe, partners. Lovers. All of it.

"As partners?" she asked cautiously, needing him to say it.

"Yes." He knelt down beside the bed so their eyes were level. "And as husband and wife. Marry me, Nia. I love you."

Tears stung her eyes, though she didn't know where her body had found the moisture. "Yes. Of course, yes. I love you, too." She clutched his fingers tight and let the fullness of it, the rightness of it surround her. And she knew one thing in her heart. "I think my father would approve."

"This isn't about him, it's about us," Rathe parroted back words she vaguely remembered throwing at him before. Then he sighed and pressed his cheek to hers. "But, yeah, I think he'd approve."

Nia closed her eyes and knew they'd just started a

new story. Their story. "The Time Nia and Rathe Saved
Boston General...
And Fell In Love."

* * * * *

*Coming in June 2005 from Harlequin Intrigue,
watch for Jessica Andersen's
steamy new medical thriller.
Logan Hart risks it all for
THE SHERIFF'S DAUGHTER
in a mystery churning with danger and desire!*

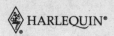

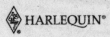

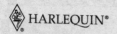

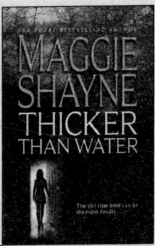

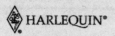